THE LUTE AND THE LIAR

Rie Sheridan Rose

DMP

2nd Edition

ISBN 978-1-77400-037-3

DEDICATION

THIS BOOK IS DEDICATED to Jonna Jackson, who was there when Digan swung his fist into Payter's nose in her living room and started the whole thing.

CHAPTER 1

MORDIGAN BRYRE GLOWERED DOWN at the boy cowering between his feet. The noonday sun beat directly down on the dusty square, sending heat waves dancing and raising the scents of baked earth and unwashed boys. They crowded around the fighters in a loose ring, thirsting for a little diversion from the workday monotony.

One fist cocked behind his shoulder, ready to strike; eyes narrowed to blazing green slits; Mordigan snarled through clenched teeth, "Take it back, you swine!"

The fallen combatant raised one arm to shield his head. His face streamed with blood in two places from Mordigan's blows. "I take it back, Digan," he burbled through a thick lip. "I take it back!"

Digan nodded his head once in emphatic satisfaction. "That's right, you do." Stepping over the boy on the ground, he scooped up the lute lying on a nearby stone wall. "I won't waste any more time with you lot. I have responsibilities. My master needs me." He tossed silky black hair out of his eyes with one strong brown hand. "I must practice. As I said, we play before the king next week."

The boy on the ground sat up shakily, drawing the back of a grimy hand across his bloodied lip. "Right. And I am the mayor," he muttered under his breath.

Digan whirled, eyes emerald fire. "Do you have something to say to me?" he purred, voice dangerously soft. The square was silent; the crowd of apprentices and shop boys holding their collective breaths to see what Payter would dare to say.

Payter's face flushed crimson. Sluggish trickles of blood still seeped from his nose and lip. "Damn it, Mordigan Bryre—somebody has got to say something!" He sprang to his feet and squared off before the taller Digan. "You are the biggest liar in the realm. You are lucky if Master Cormeyer allows you to carry his instrument into the castle—much less perform before the king!"

Digan's fist flew up, the lute clutched white-knuckle tight in his other hand. He stepped toward Payter then dropped his arm. "You aren't worth the trouble."

With an imperious sniff of disdain, Digan swept his cape about him and stalked away from the square, head held high.

I mustn't let them see how much it hurts. They will make much of Payter, won't they? Think he's won the day for standing up to me. Well, they won't get the satisfaction of thinking I care. I won't look back and see them crowing over me. I won't!

Digan didn't look back. Digan never looked back.

Mordigan Bryre was seventeen. His parents died when he was a mere babe of two, leaving him in the desultory care of an old woman dwelling on the outskirts of the town. Sometime later, Cormeyer Stareyes, the King's Bard, discovered four-year-old Digan playing with a homemade lyre in the dirt of this very square. Digan remembered well the widow's eagerness to agree when Cormeyer offered to take the boy into his service.

That long-ago day changed the boy's future. Digan was apprenticed to the bard on the spot, and for the last thirteen summers, his life had revolved around his music. He learned his lessons well, living and breathing for the art that sustained him.

Tall and slender, with the strong yet delicate hands of a true musician, Digan's ebony hair and emerald eyes caught the attention of many an eye. The green and black garments he favored set off these attributes to excellent advantage, as well he knew. There was only one flaw in the package: a glib tongue that was as quick to invent a tall tale as tell the truth.

Mordigan Bryre was an inveterate liar. Falsehoods poured from his mouth like water. It was the only serious fault he was ever beaten for and not even repeated canings could break him of the habit. His quick temper and flying fists made certain that most of his companions pretended to accept his stories, however. Usually.

Today, when Digan claimed that he would soon become a journeyman and play his own music before the king, Payter was brave enough to protest. And the galling thing—the thing that made Digan knock the smaller boy to the ground—was that, for once, he was telling the truth.

Digan's heart soared instinctively with the memory of that morning's audience.

He knocked softly on Cormeyer's office door when he received the summons, wondering uneasily what the

Master Bard would find fault with on this occasion.

"Ah, Mordigan—there you are." Cormeyer looked up from a sheaf of music and waved him to a seat before the parchment-strewn desk. "I have been reviewing your composition, my boy. Very impressive for a lad of your years. You have studied hard, Mordigan, and when you apply yourself, you have an admirable talent. It is rough, and needs much polish, but shows promise."

Digan felt his face flush with pleasure. Compliments from Cormeyer were few and far between. It always seemed that the master's kind words were more often gifted on the other apprentices while Cormeyer waxed more critical than ever when it came to Digan's work.

Secretly, the boy often wondered if the bard might have a personal reason for plucking him off the streets, but he dared not broach the subject with his stern master.

"I think it is time, perhaps, to reward that promise," Cormeyer continued. "Do you realize that a fortnight from now marks your fourteenth full year here in the Hall? You will be eighteen, and I believe it is high time that you progress to journeyman status."

"Oh, sir! Shall I really get my papers?"

Cormeyer's dark brows drew together in a warning frown. "That depends entirely upon you, Mordigan Bryre. A bard must be able to curb his tongue when expedient, flatter when he must, and never be seen to lose his composure when provoked. You must be diplomat and arbiter. Frankly, it is in these aspects I fear you lack the most. Keep yourself out of trouble until the day, and we shall see what we shall see. Now..."

Cormeyer next picked up a sheet of music—Digan's own music—and nodded approvingly. "This piece is very nice. *Easy to finger, yet the melody has hidden complexity. I would like to introduce it at next week's court concert. What say you, Digan—would you like to play it with me before the king? You can easily perform this recorder part, and it would be a nice showcase for you."*

"*I shall play before the king?*" Digan was stunned. He often sang for King Vasileios' court, but his voice was his greatest talent. To play before the court was an altogether different thing. "*I—I am honored, Master.*"

"*As well you should be.*" Cormeyer rose to his feet, one of the few men Digan needed to look up to, and clasped the boy's shoulder in a rare gesture of affection. "*You deserve the honor,*" he continued, his voice warm. "*Now prove to me that you can accept it gracefully. Curb that temper of yours under a tight rein, and we'll see how you ride.*" The Stareyes Clan were originally horsemen from the Upper Plateaus, and Cormeyer's allusions still tended toward the equestrian.

Well, now I've gone and fallen off the horse again, Digan thought, with a rueful grimace. *I just hope I can placate the master without losing the honor that led to the scuffle in the first place.* But Payter would pick today to challenge him...and Digan couldn't stand idly by and be ridiculed, could he?

It started off well enough when Digan decided to steal a few minutes on his way between shop and Hall to tell his friends the news. Digan retrieved his master's lute with plenty of time to spare before Princess Allysian's lesson, but when he entered the south end of the square and saw Garad and Sult lounging by the central fountain, he couldn't resist stopping to boast of his good fortune.

Garad, newly ensconced in the Cadet barracks at the City Watch complex, was suitably impressed by what such an honor could mean, but Sult's indifference was the first irritant of the day.

"Well enough," yawned Sult, indolently arranging his long limbs in such a manner as to show off a new tunic to best advantage. It was an instinctive habit in the player's apprentice, much as Digan would unconsciously finger an imaginary instrument when bored or frustrated. "But I don't see what all the fuss is about," continued the other. "It's not as if you have never performed at court, Digan. You have been showcased more times than I can count."

There was a hint of envy in the off-hand remark that went a long way towards soothing Digan's ruffled feathers. Sult had a fine speaking voice of his own, and was an adroit mimic, but he couldn't sing a note, a skill he ardently coveted.

Garad, ever the peace-maker, stepped in before Digan could overreact with a smooth, "That's splendid, Digan. What will you play?"

"A new air composed for recorder and lute," replied Digan proudly, "and I am the composer."

A nasty little voice sneered, "Go on! Tell another. The king has better to do than listen to caterwauling like you wring from that wooden stick." Payter had arrived unnoticed, and now leaned against the fountain, arms folded across his skinny chest.

Digan began to strum the lute as he walked through the bustling streets, fingers moving with absent-minded skill to send freshets of music tumbling into the busy stalls. Several heads cocked, conversations dying to whispers as he passed, then renewing with lighter tones behind him. His technical playing was faultless, but it was not what made Digan's music so beautiful. The bright soul behind it shone through his gravest faults.

He soon left the crowded market behind as he crossed out of the square proper, though he could hear the vague roar of it at his back. Marineaux was a well-ordered kingdom, and the thoughtful planning of its capital city reflected the same.

The central core of the town proper was laid out with precision, a greater square of shops and alleys surrounding the market itself. Each section of the outer square catered to its own clientele, and a stranger was easily directed to their needs.

As Digan strolled south towards the Guild Hall, he passed between the Crafter's Corner and the quarter known as "Rich Man's Run." From the one came the mouth-watering aroma of fresh bread from the baker's guild, and from the other the sound of early revelers drinking at the Trivial Pursuits Gaming Den. On another day, he might have loitered outside the tavern. His playing often put coins in his pockets when he passed this way, but today he was later than he should be.

Master Cormeyer will have my head if I cause him to lose face before the princess. I should never have wasted time in the square. If I hurry, I might be able to make up the time...

The passing thought sped up his feet for a time, but gradually, he slowed again as he passed the Academy. The sing-song monotony of the students chanting their lessons drifted through the open windows, and stirred a brief spasm of envy in Digan's heart, but he shrugged it away.

I was not meant for study. I know my scales, and I can scribe the proper notation for my scores. What more do I need? What care I for words scribbled on parchment? I keep my lyrics in my head where they are safe.

Digan crossed out of the merchant's square and continued along the broad central avenue towards the city wall, his feet moving a little faster again. Beyond this larger heart, the body of the town sprawled with greater abandon, but even the poorest sections of houses had refuse channels in the streets, and width enough for two horses to ride abreast on the main roadways.

Nodding to the sentries on duty, Digan hurried through the massive city gates.

"Sing us a tune, Digan!" called one of the guards as he passed. "You know the one I like—that one about the barmaid and the unicorn."

"Not today, Casdan. I am late enough already." He waved an apology.

"Come back this evening for it then."

"I'll do my best."

Digan was popular among the soldiers for his sharp wit and wide repertoire of bawdy ballads. Garad was a cadet with the Guard, and often teased Digan about joining up, but Mordigan was quite content with life as it was.

Despite his greater speed, his fingers continued to dance across the strings of the lute, and his heart lifted. Soon his pace slowed once more, savoring the music as he strolled through the trees framing the road. The Guild Hall was situated a half mile outside of the town proper, and the walk was a pleasant one, despite the heat.

The sound of a lute always helped him calm his anger, and Master Cormeyer's instrument was a truly splendid piece of craftsmanship. Digan hummed along with the melody he played, and then began to sing softly in his fine tenor.

Whither dost thou wander,
lady, in the heather?
The spring of youth has faded...
and the winter chill
is nigh...
Dost thou still remember,
the days we spent together?
When love was fresh as roses...
and no storm cloud
brushed the sky...

"What a lovely melody," crooned a cracked voice from the side of the road. Digan jumped. Lost in his song, he was startled to find someone else was nearby. "And how true the words," continued the voice with a mournful sigh.

Clutching the lute before him with both hands, like a talisman, Digan glanced wildly about, searching for the unknown speaker. His eye fell on a bundle of rags lying beside the road, and he gasped as the pile resolved itself into a wrinkled old woman with a gnarled staff. He knew that figure—all within the realm knew of her—but he had hoped never to make her acquaintance.

Her tattered black robes fluttered about her, whitened with road dust where they had lain against the ground. The relentless sun drew shades of rust and bottle-fly green from the drapes and folds of the black garment.

She must be sweltering in all that heavy velvet—I am stifling in this lighter tunic. But perhaps such a mighty witch like Freitanya does not feel the heat...perhaps she can spell even the weather. 'Tis rumored that she is more powerful even than the legendary Talthos. She is not one to be trifled with...or denied. Late or not, I cannot risk affronting her.

Digan gave her his best courtier's bow, sweeping off his green velvet cap as he did so. "T-thank you, my lady. High praise indeed from one of your stature."

Freitanya limped forward, leaning heavily on her staff. "Have we met before, boy?"

"I don't think so," Digan frowned, some vague fancy tugging at his memory. It was gone before he could catch it, but it took with it much of his fear. "I think I would remember."

"Perhaps it was your father..."

"Then it was long ago, for he is dead these fifteen years."

"And what do they call you, boy?"

"My name is Mordigan Bryre, bard to the king." The lie slipped out unbidden.

"Young you are to be King's Bard...and I thought Cormeyer Stareyes still owned that title." Freitanya began to circle around him.

Digan gulped, and turned with her, striving to keep the lute firmly wedged between them. "Well...I am to—to take Cormeyer's place after the festival next month. He decided to retire to the country and tutor privately. I will assume his court duties...it is a challenge for one so young, but I feel I am equipped for it." His chin lifted, defying her to gainsay his claim.

She reached forward and squeezed his arm. "No doubt you are," she murmured in a thoughtful tone, still circling him. "No doubt you are."

"M-master Cormeyer is expecting me to meet him. I am already late..." That much at least was true.

Her twisted fingers moved to brush against the strings of the lute. A soft, sweet chord rang in the air then died away. "A beautiful instrument," Freitanya commented.

"Y-yes. It was commissioned for my master by the king's father..." His voice died in his throat when he remembered whom it had been commissioned *from*. There was said to be no love lost between the wizard and the witch.

"Talthos could be a master craftsman when he chose to be. I feel the power in this piece. Do you?"

"What do you mean, lady?" Digan frowned, studying the lute with anxious suspicion. It was carved from rosewood, inlaid with ivory and gold—a valuable instrument, to be sure—but nothing particularly out of the ordinary, even to his trained eye. *Is there something wrong with the instrument? Did they damage it at the shop? I don't see anything different about it...*

"No. You do not feel the magic. Perhaps it is for the best. For a boy like you—"

Digan straightened to his full height, back arched in offended dignity. "I am no mere boy, lady! I am a man full-grown...or nearly so. And a journeyman bard—"

"What?" she scoffed, "not 'the King's Bard' now, but a mere journeyman?"

Digan scowled, his cheeks darkening beneath their smooth tan. He had forgotten his earlier boast in the heat of the moment, but it hurt him to hear the truth made light of. It was no dishonor to be a journeyman at eighteen.

Freitanya cackled at his aggrieved expression. "Too easily wounded, little bird. Smooth your ruffled feathers. I merely meant that a boy—your pardon." She sketched a mocking bow. "A *young man*—of your upbringing might be no match for magic. It takes long training to properly employ enchantment in one not born to it. But oh..." Her fingers coaxed another chord from the taut strings. "...What wondrous music could a true master bring forth with a lute such as this one."

A passionate desire surged through Digan's breast, until it ached to catch his breath. "I shall become that master, lady! Tell me but how!"

The witch squinted up at him—one eye squeezed nearly shut, the other a bright black bead. "I doubt you have the stomach for it, boy. The hunger, yes; perhaps the will...but the nerve—ah, that's another story."

"Are you calling me coward?" asked Digan softly, in the voice that sent the shop boys running for cover from his wrath. Despite his caution toward the witch, he found himself ready to defend his bravery, stepping forward to tower over her without conscious thought.

"So...the chick has an eaglet's talons, does it?" the witch crowed, her voice gleeful. "Perhaps you do possess the courage. It would be an interesting test..."

His honor was at stake now. "Set me your test. I am not afraid! I would learn how to master the magic of the lute."

"This isn't even your lute, boy. Should we not let Cormeyer say if you 'master' his instrument?"

Digan bowed his head. Freitanya was right—the lute was not his to play. He was only in possession of it now because Cormeyer broke a peg last evening and was too busy to take it for repair this morning. One of the journeymen left it at The Harp and Horn for Master Egletine's handiwork and Digan was sent to fetch it when it was ready. He was supposed to return to the Hall with it hours ago.

If I edged around the witch, could I run for home?

As if sensing his thoughts, Freitanya laid a gnarled hand on his arm. The touch sent a spark of power through him, and he shivered.

"How badly do you crave the magic, boy? What will you dare to risk?" queried Freitanya—and her voice lost all its aged huskiness, melting into liquid silver. He stared into dark, rain-gray eyes that swallowed his soul, laying bare the darkest secrets and hidden passions of his dreams. A faint whiff of sun-warmed oranges wafted from her tumbled cloud of fine white hair. The scent seemed strangely young for one of her venerable years.

"What must I do?" he breathed.

"You do have a gift," she murmured in that thoughtful tone he sensed before. "With the aid of magic, that seed of talent could flourish...but you will have to face many trials—and risk much. Do you want it fiercely enough?"

"More than anything in the world, lady..."

"We shall see about that. First, you will have to make a solemn vow—you can inform no one of this meeting between we two. To do so will have dire consequences."

"As you wish, lady."

"Secondly, you will not be able to claim the magic of another. You must go and petition Talthos for a lute of your own."

"But Talthos is dead."

"No. He has merely forsaken this realm. He lives above the clouds in a castle of azure stone. It is a long and arduous journey...if you have the grit for it. And there is one further demand required for the successful completion of this quest."

"What demand is that?"

The witch seemed to grow in stature. Her eyes glowed with intensity, and Digan trembled with an uncontrollable shiver. "If you stray from the truth— even the slightest bit—you will begin to lose that lovely voice of yours. The greater the lie, the worse the loss...and the longer it will last. If the lie is great enough—your voice will be gone forever, and the quest will be in vain."

Digan's hand faltered to his throat in an involuntary gesture. He gulped. His voice was his only true asset. It was his chief vanity as well as his livelihood. *To risk the loss of my speech would be hard indeed...but oh, to gain such magic!*

"I accept your conditions," he croaked, desire winning over caution. "Just...please, what must I do?"

"Go on to your appointment, boy. Meet your master, as planned. And remember your vows. A signpost will appear at the proper time to show you the way forward—you will know it." She limped away down the road with a cackle of laughter. As Digan turned to continue on his own way, she called back over her shoulder, "Remember, boy! Speak only the truth!" With a final wicked trill of laughter, she vanished.

Digan slung the lute across his back by its broad leather strap, and began to run. Already late when Freitanya stopped him, he would be in serious trouble now.

The Master will be furious. He sent me for the instrument because he had other duties before the Princess Allysian's this afternoon. By being late, not only do I waste his time, but embarrass him before the princess as well.

Digan sighed, lengthening his stride and fairly flying down the road. The chalky white dust of the roadbed puffed about his feet like snow, graying his leggings and boots. He mopped his brow on one pleated sleeve, darkening the emerald silk of his best shirt. "By Hastor's Harp, I must look a fright," he groaned aloud, "and the master will cane me for sure this time. I should have been back hours ago." *If I take full blame, Allysian will not hold it against Cormeyer...but he will beat me for it regardless. Ah well, nothing for it.*

At least Cormeyer only rarely resorts to the cane, which is more than can be said for most of the other masters in town. My friends are not all so lucky.

The apprentice skidded to a stop in the paved courtyard outside the Music Hall. Hands braced on his knees, he hung his head, fighting to catch his breath.

Mordigan sagged back against the warm stone of the Hall, feeling the rough texture even through his velvet doublet. It was security; it was strength; it was home. The two-story structure towered over him, its sandstone blocks buttery gold in the sunlight. Ivy climbed the walls in sprawling profusion, providing many a daredevil with precarious access to the gently pitched tiles of the slate roof. The octagonal Hall housed nearly two dozen apprentices and half again as many journeymen, under the tutelage of Cormeyer and three other masters.

From where he stood, Digan could hear the sound of choral practice in the main rehearsal chamber through the open doorway. He winced as Starsen hit his obligatory flat note, and heard the patient murmur of Master Bertine instructing the boy to start again. Starsen was attempting to fill in for Digan himself, but his range was not up to the challenge.

Digan sighed. *That will add a stripe or two to my back. Cormeyer hates for me to miss a practice, whether I need it or not.*

He beat off the worst of the chalk dust with his cap, and set it back upon his head at a rakish angle. Then, feigning an indifference he did not feel, he sauntered through the ornate arched doorway and into the Hall, the lute in hand.

After the heat and relentless brilliance of the summer sun, the cool darkness of the interior was a mixed blessing. Mordigan shivered as the sweat evaporated beneath his doublet.

The corridor was lit only by widely spaced candle sconces and long windows high in the storage bays sandwiched between the floors. The dim light picked out broad wooden benches standing against the wainscoting, and the tall cabinets where the musical scores were stored. He could hear the continuing choral practice to his left in the central chamber, and now that he was inside the Hall, he could hear one of the journeymen playing the lap harp somewhere down the corridor. *Laeran, most like. There is that delicacy to the sound that is his special gift. He will be receiving his master's brooch soon, I warrant.*

The familiar scents of beeswax and lemon oil rose from the polished furniture in a comforting cloud as Digan took a deep breath to calm his thudding heart. Despite his affected nonchalance, he hated to disappoint Master Cormeyer, and he knew that the bard was going to be furious.

He squared his shoulders and pushed open the door to Cormeyer's private study. The room was a familiar jumble of ordered chaos. Sheaves of score sheets were scattered across the long table dominating one wall, and filed in the cubbyholes above the desk angled into the far corner. A floor harp stood opposite the long table beside a large window. Sunlight streamed across the floor, highlighting the gilding on the instrument. The scent of roses wafted through the open casement to perfume the room. Digan glanced around the room for his master.

"So, my boy—you finally deign to favor us with

your presence," purred the bard. One of the most successful lessons that Cormeyer had taught Mordigan was that deceptive drawl which warned the listener the speaker was in no trifling mood. "How kind of you!" Cormeyer practically ripped the instrument out of Digan's hand, turning away and beginning to tune it with an ostentatious flourish.

Watching the master's broad back as he adjusted the new peg on the lute, Digan felt the old pang of longing knife through him. With his dark hair, shot through now with silver, and tall frame, many people mistook Cormeyer Stareyes for Mordigan's father upon first acquaintance.

As a boy, Digan sometimes wondered if this was the truth of his parentage, but he remembered well the day Cormeyer, in a moment of rare expansiveness, gently assured him it was not the case.

He was in the courtyard, snuffling quietly in a corner and trying to hide tears engendered by a group of the older boys teasing him for being an orphan.

"I am not!" he declared to his tormentors. "I belong to Master Cormeyer!"

"Belong, maybe. I hear he bought you in the market like a pet dog."

Digan flailed out at the boy, and received a bloodied nose and derisive laughter for his troubles.

Now, he was trying to get himself under control so that he could return to the Hall.

"Mordigan," came a quiet voice behind him.

He turned, to find the Master standing in the shadows. He swiped a hand across his eyes, and put on a brave front. "Yes, sir?"

"I hear you had a bit of a scrap today, my lad."

Digan hung his head. "Yes, sir."

Cormeyer came and hunkered down before the boy, laying a hand on his shoulder. "I am not your father, child. I wish I could give you that comfort, but it would be crueler in the end. You are a good lad." He brushed the hair out of Digan's eyes with a gentle hand. "I know it is hard for you to be without a family of your own. But I cannot let you live the lie."

It all comes down to lies, it seems. One way or the other, I cannot seem to get away from them...

Hanging his head, Digan noticed out of the corner of his eye that Allysian was already present, quietly strumming her own lute and pretending to study a sheet of music, her long blond hair swinging forward to hide her face. As if feeling his gaze upon her, she glanced up, cool blue eyes meeting his own stormy green, and he quickly transferred his focus back to the ground before him.

"Where have you been, Mordigan?" asked Cormeyer in that same silken growl, his back still turned to the boy.

"Oh, sir! You won't believe! I—" Digan faltered to a stop in confusion. He suddenly realized that he could not lie, or he would risk the curse—but he could not reveal the truth, or he would break his vow not to speak of his meeting with Freitanya. He remained silent.

"Yes? What will I not believe?" Cormeyer set the lute upon the composition table, turning to Digan at last. He favored the boy with a frowning scowl, dark eyes hooded beneath the beetling brows.

"Nothing, sir," Digan mumbled.

"You are right. I will not believe 'nothing.' Now, tell me where you have been!"

"I—I stopped in the square."

"Yes, I know," nodded Cormeyer, "Payter's father dragged him down and exhibited the bruises. We will discuss that matter later—but that was near an hour gone. Where have you been since you left the square? Even you should have traveled that distance in a shorter time."

Digan flushed. He bore a reputation for laziness when he could get away with it, and knew, to his shame, that it was not entirely undeserved. He was good at conceiving ways to dodge his chores. "I came as quickly as I could," he mumbled.

The statement was not entirely true, and Digan's throat tightened in a painful contraction. It was his first taste of the witch's curse, and he felt a thrill of fear. The words were only a slight exaggeration. What would it feel like if he *really* lied?

Cormeyer sighed and moved to the desk. He picked up a sheet of parchment, glancing down at it. He scrubbed his hand across his face, a habit of his when troubled. "Mordigan, do you know what this is?"

"No, sir."

"This is your journeyman's certification. It states that you have the knowledge and skills required by the Guild charter to claim the rights and privileges of the rank." He leaned back against the desk. "Do you think that you have earned it?"

"I have passed all the tests, sir," Digan replied, confused by the question.

"True. But have you earned the rank?"

"I don't understand."

"There is more to being a bard than technical expertise on the instruments, lad. It is a sacred trust. Do you know why we have an affiliation with the Runner's Guild?"

"No, sir."

"Because a bard is considered to be a bearer of news as well as entertainment. He is expected to pass on new edicts to the countryside. He is trusted to carry important messages between the king and his lords; between villages; between homesteads with no other access to each other. How can I say that you are qualified to be a journeyman when you cannot even be trusted on a simple errand? When you lie your way out of every difficult situation?" He lay the precious document down in the center of the cluttered desk.

Digan opened his mouth to protest, but there was nothing to be said in his own defense.

Across the room, Allysian fingered the strings of her lute, humming the chords softly as she worked on the correct positioning. She appeared to be oblivious of the argument, but Digan was all too painfully aware of her presence. It made his disgrace that much harder to bear.

Allysian bowed her head over her music and watched the confrontation between Digan and Master Cormeyer through hooded lashes. She worried a great deal about Mordigan Bryre. Truth be told, the boy took up far more of her thoughts than their level of acquaintance merited.

She knew full well how proud Digan was...and

how deucedly stubborn. *He will never be able to admit it to Master Cormeyer if loitering in the square with his friends—or, worse yet, flirting with some girl—is the cause of his tardiness.* Allysian bit her lip in vexation. *He can't be late because of that...even the thought of Digan dallying with a sweetheart among the townsfolk...*

The thought tightened Allysian's chest, and made her want to burst into tears.

That isn't very fair of me either, I know. After all, Digan is seventeen now, and he bears a man's responsibilities here at the Guild Hall. If only he could hear how Master Cormeyer was boasting about him before he burst in so unaccountably late. Bragging about how he would get his journeyman's papers in a few days.

Digan will no longer be simply a lowly apprentice. He might even be sent away to study under another bard for a time...

No! I refuse to let it come to that. I will concoct some scheme to keep that disaster from befalling. I will use all my ingenuity to keep Digan here at the Hall. Of course, Papa will explode if he ever learns the truth of how I feel about this penniless orphan, but I am accustomed to dealing with his temper.

Allysian only vaguely remembered a time when she wasn't secretly in love with Mordigan Bryre. Of course, she confided that fact to no one—especially not the absolutely impossible Digan.

She took full advantage of the fact Master Cormeyer was berating the boy to indulge in her favorite pastime—staring at Mordigan Bryre. Allysian tried not to be too obvious about it, but she just couldn't seem to help herself. *Something about that thin, narrow face of his, with its piercing green eyes, fascinates me. Well, if I am being perfectly honest,* everything *about it fascinates me.*

Watching Digan instead of her fingering, she struck a jangling discord, and both musicians glanced at her instinctively. She felt the blood rush to her cheeks as she bent over her lute—but not before she caught Digan's eye lingering on her for an instant longer than entirely necessary, the ghost of a smile on his lips.

Her heart sang, and Allysian stored the fleeting glimpse in the corner of her memory where she hoarded such incidents. *When we were younger, it was so much easier to collect the odd smile or friendly snatch of conversation from Digan, but the two year gap in our ages seemed to widen over time, or perhaps it is just our relative positions are different now. Of course, I was always a princess, but I suppose it is easier for a seven-year-old boy to overlook that fact than a youth of seventeen...*

After her mother died in childbirth, her father had raised her alone. It made their relationship a very strong one, but it also made Allysian a bit young for her age—unschooled in the womanly arts most of her contemporaries took for granted. She knew this, and tried to act more grown up and responsible, but knowing that it was necessary didn't make it easier to do.

She settled the green apple silk of her dress into smoother folds about her lap. *I wore this particular gown because of Digan's fondness for green. He told me once that he liked it. I wonder if he'll even notice?*

Master Cormeyer slammed his fist down on the edge of the desk, making her jump, and she turned her concentration back to the matter at hand. *What trouble will Digan get himself into now?*

Cormeyer slammed his fist down on the edge of the desk. "Speak up, boy. I grow weary of these games!" The master's voice was beginning to rise in volume and intensity.

Digan gulped. His hands felt clammy with tension, and his throat was dry. *What can I say to him to turn his wrath? I've never seen him so angry.* Digan steeled himself for whatever was to come. *I'm in for more than a light caning this time.*

Mouth working without success for several seconds, Mordigan finally managed to stammer, "I-I can't tell you, sir. I promised I would not." He twisted his cap nervously in his hands. He tried to convey through his melodious voice his sincere desire to obey his master's command without angering Cormeyer further, but Digan could see at once that the attempt was in vain. Shoulders sagging in defeat, he waited for his punishment.

Thank Hathor the others are at rehearsal. He could not bear it if the entire Hall were to witness this humiliation. It is disgrace enough that Allysian should see me scolded like a child.

Cormeyer ran both hands through his thick hair, turning his back on the boy and dropping his head. A sigh rumbled from the center of his chest to stir the papers on the desk. "This is the last straw, Mordigan Bryre. You are a talented boy, but you are no genius." He paced across the room, running a hand over the strings of the standing harp. His hand lingered on the frame of the instrument, as if needing the support.

For the first time, Digan realized the master was no longer a young man. He knew the king's father as a journeyman, and became King's Bard before Allysian's birth. His large frame seemed to have shrunk in the last few minutes. The handsome burgundy doublet was hiked up on one side of his belt, but he did not seem to notice its disarray. That in itself was unusual for the normally fastidious master.

Squaring his shoulders, Cormeyer turned to Digan, his brown eyes grave. "Perhaps if you were a genius I could forgive you such rampant insolence and erratic behavior...but you are not. I tried to teach you to be a good man as well as an adequate musician. It appears that I failed. I am tired of dealing with your tantrums, your lies, your incessant fighting, and your irresponsibility. Pack your things at once and get out. You are no longer apprenticed here." He strode to the desk and swept up the journeyman's certificate. With one deliberate gesture, he ripped the parchment in half, dropping the pieces to the desk, and then turned to Digan, arms folded across his broad chest.

Digan's jaw fell open. He stared in stunned silence at Cormeyer. *Surely it is but a jest—the master cannot be serious...* "B-but I turn eighteen in less than two weeks' time! You promised—"

"You have not earned the honor of becoming a journeyman. This latest incident just goes to prove you are not fit for such responsibility. I overlooked your shortcomings time and again. No more. Your behavior disappointed my expectations for the last time. There is nothing more for you here. Leave as soon as you gather your things." Cormeyer turned his back on Mordigan, and moved across to where Allysian sat beside the doorway.

Digan could hardly breathe.

His world was collapsing.

Without my journeyman's papers, I can never rise to full bard, and I know no other trade. I will never find a responsible position unless I earn a bard's title. Without my papers, I won't even be able to legally accept wages to play. I am not skilled with my hands. I learned no craft but music. I have no schooling... How will I make my way in the world?

His head swam. His breath caught in his chest. *What am I to do?* Panic welled within him. He took a step toward Cormeyer, taking a breath to protest the injustice of the dismissal.

At that moment, the princess glanced up at Digan, sky-blue eyes filled with compassionate pity, and then turned back to her music as Cormeyer returned to her interrupted lesson.

Digan felt his face grow hot. The disgrace stung all the more because she witnessed it. Her compassion only made things worse. Anger swallowed his panic. *For Cormeyer to dishonor me before the princess is an unnecessary cruelty. The dismissal itself is disgrace enough.*

Allysian was a sympathetic soul of fifteen, and Digan's admiration of her independent spirit went back to childhood. To be ousted in her presence made him feel even more like an errant child. The anger smoldered in his breast like a hot coal.

I will not let Cormeyer see how devastated I feel. I

cannot. I must be brave and put a good face on it.

Steeling himself, Digan drew upon every ounce of dignity and courage he possessed and turned to Cormeyer. "I am sorry that I failed you, Master. Perhaps someday I will regain your esteem." Not daring to look over at the princess where she sat in the corner, he strode to the doorway.

"Wait, boy," grunted Cormeyer.

Digan's heart rejoiced. *I knew it! The master but jested. Now he will forgive me, and scold me roughly not to let it happen again—throwing in a cuff or two to drive the message home...* "Yes, master?" He hated the lift of hope in his voice. It made him sound needy.

Cormeyer stepped up beside him, laying a callused hand upon his shoulder in a rare gesture of affection that seemed out of place considering the circumstances, and slipped him a handful of small silver. "For your expenses. Godspeed."

Digan stared down at the coins in his hand.

If I were brave enough, I would fling them to the floor and stalk out—but if I am truly being cast out, they might be my only buffer against starvation.

He swallowed hard. "Thank you, Master," he whispered, his voice dull and lifeless. "I-I won't be taking anything else."

Squaring his shoulders, he left the Music Hall. Pausing at the front doorway, he looked down the broad, chalk road. One direction led back into the town proper, but he would find no comfort there. Taking a deep breath, Digan turned away from the capital and started down the long road curving away toward the far horizon.

Allysian jerked back to the reality of the moment with a crash as Cormeyer issued the stunning command that Digan pack his things and leave the Hall. Feeling the blood drain from her face, she started to her feet in automatic protest, and then sat back down with a thump. The room was growing oddly gray around the edges, and she was suddenly giddy.

Speechless to protest, she watched Digan gather his composure and stride out of the chamber. Her mind was numb. *What can I do? How can I stop this?*

Master Cormeyer turned to her after the boy left, pointing to a section of her music. "Begin here, my lady, and play to this measure." His voice was steady, but Allysian thought she detected a roughness to the tone.

Why is he pretending that it doesn't matter? Digan is like his own son. How can he send him away like this?

Her fingers fumbled on the strings, feeling like leaden sticks as she tried valiantly to comply. All she could think about was the fact that Mordigan was being sent away from her. *I will lose even the slim comfort of seeing him at these weekly lessons. I cannot let that happen.*

Under the assault of her clumsy fingers, a string on Allysian's lute snapped with a tortured twang. "I-I'll fetch another," she murmured, leaping to her feet before Cormeyer could dissuade her, and bolting from the Hall.

The full skirts of her gown billowed about her feet like windswept water. *Damn these skirts! Why must fashion favor such a stupid excess of material? Papa says it is calculated to keep a woman staid and proper. Well, fie on that!*

Gathering her skirts in both hands she wadded the silk into bunches, hiking it up out of her way. She was heedless of the wrinkles she was crushing into the tissue-thin fabric.

Reaching the road, she stared wildly from side to side until she spied the tall figure trudging away from town. Heart rising into her throat at the sight of him, she pelted off down the road, long hair tangling in the breeze.

"Digan!" she shouted, breathless from her dash. "Wait! Please!"

He stopped, and turned, giving her an opportunity to catch up.

Allysian slid to a stop beside him. Her delicate satin slippers, originally a shade darker than the apple of her dress, were now almost ivory with the dust of the road. Her feet skidded on the sharp pebbles, and she reached out a hand automatically to steady herself, catching his arm. He braced her up, and then dropped her hand as if stung.

"Y-you mustn't go," she mumbled, hiding behind the veil of her hair as she studied the ground between them. "Master Cormeyer is merely angry. He will be sorry in time. If you tell him where you were, and give him a chance—"

"I can't tell him. I promised a lady."

The words confirmed her worst fears, and she felt her face grow hot. "So, dallying with some girl is worth losing your place?" she accused, her voice waspish with injured pride.

He looked away from her, staring down the long empty road ahead of him. "All I have is my honor, Your

Highness," he replied softly, "and I gave my oath."

Allysian searched the grave features before her. She saw them through a film of tears that blurred the familiar outlines into something mysterious. "But where will you go, Digan?" she whispered. "How... when will you come back?"

Mordigan shrugged. "Maybe I won't. There is nothing to keep me here, after all."

"Nothing?" The word was almost a sob. *By the Seven Virgins, I wish I could swallow that back again!*

The clod doesn't appear to have noticed. Will he force me to tell him plain?

"This is a chance for me to see the world," he responded, with an airy gesture at the far horizon. "To make my fortune. Perhaps it's for the best."

Allysian felt her eyes fill with tears, and willed them not to fall.

Digan lifted her chin and smiled down at her. "Cheer up, Princess. One would think that you will miss me. Don't worry your pretty little head. You will forget you knew me by winter."

She shook that head violently— flinging tears into the dust— and snatched a heavy golden comb out of her honey-colored tresses, heedless of the strands of hair ripped out with it. "Never, Mordigan Bryre. Never." A bit surprised by her own effrontery, she threw her arms around his waist and buried her hot face against his chest. "I will never forget you," she wailed miserably. Then, shoving the comb into his hand without another word, she pulled away from him and ran toward home as fast as her feet would carry her.

Mordigan stared after Allysian's fleeing form with a pensive longing. Her sob was *not* unnoticed...but duty bade him ignore it.

She is a sweet child, and always given to displays of affection I could once accept, but know I must now discourage. She is also a princess, and as far above my station as the clouds drifting overhead.

Digan sighed. *No matter. My present circumstances need evaluation, not the past. I don't know where I should go...life with Master Cormeyer is all I remember...I recall only the vaguest impressions of my life before my apprenticeship began. With one sweeping decree, I've lost both home and family—such as it was. I fear I shall have cause to damn the pride that prohibited me from returning to my room for what scant possessions I own. Here I am, thrust upon the road with only the clothes on my back and a handful of small silver—not enough to live on for more than a week or two at best, no matter how carefully I stretch it. Oh, and whatever this is that Allysian thrust upon me.*

He glanced down at the object in his hand, then whistled, and brought it up to his eye to examine more closely. The comb was an intricately woven knot of gold strands on a gilt base. It weighed several ounces, and was probably worth a goodly sum.

I must see that it is returned to her someday—it is far too valuable for me to keep...but it is a typically generous gesture on her part.

Digan slipped the comb inside his belt pouch and started walking once more, his head down as he contemplated what just occurred. The princess' odd behavior preoccupied his thoughts.

Whatever possessed her to give me the comb? And what did that choked sob indicate? Does she fancy...no— she is a princess. She didn't mean...

He was so distracted by his musings that he never heard them coming. Suddenly, someone shoved him violently from behind, and he fell headlong to the stony road, sliding several feet on his face before he could stop himself and roll over. The dust of the road rose in a choking cloud about him, and the air was heavy with the dry smell of chalk. He coughed and spat. As he twisted around, trying to catch a glimpse of his assailant, he met a hard kick in the ribs, and doubled in on the pain, letting slip an involuntary moan.

"Not so high-and-mighty now, are you?" snarled a voice made unrecognizable by hatred.

Digan pushed himself up to his hands and knees and peered up at the speaker through a tangled curtain of hair. It was Payter, one eye blackened and lip still swollen from Digan's earlier blows. "What do you want?" Digan muttered, pretending a bravado he did not feel.

"You'll see soon enough." Payter nodded his head.

A chill of fear ran through Digan. *Sweet Hathor... he's not alone. This will be no fair fight.*

The realization came too late to be of use. As Digan dove for the side of the road, two new assailants grabbed him from behind. They jerked him to his feet, pinning his arms securely—and painfully— behind his back. The boys who held him were much larger than Payter, and smelled like they frequently rolled in horse manure.

Most likely the stable boys from the Kettle. Trust

Payter to run to the bullies. He dare not fight me alone.

He caught a confused impression of dun homespun and patched leggings, but was unable to turn far enough to see their faces.

One of them leaned down to his ear, breathing a foul combination of garlic and onion into his face as he whispered, "This were too good an opportunity to pass up, my lad. I've heard the songs you sing about me on the square with those jackdaw friends of yours." He kneed Digan sharply in the small of the back, and Digan bit back a cry.

Yes, I know that voice. The stupid lout was mooning over Matilde at the Traveler's Rest, *the pretty, brunette chambermaid Garad is so sweet on. The song he refers to was one of my better ballads, and well received by both the girl and the cadet. Unfortunately, it appears its appeal is not universal.*

"I've been waiting for this for a long time, Mordigan Bryre," Payter crowed, with a wicked sneer. He slammed his fist into Digan's midsection, and the taller boy doubled over, the wind knocked out of him.

"How does it feel, getting for giving?" Payter growled. "Where's your high-blown boasting now?"

The pair of oafs holding Digan shook him like a rat, knocking him off balance. He swayed to find his equilibrium once more. He could taste bile in the back of his throat, and the acid tang of fear, but he was determined not to show it.

"Is that the best you can do?" Digan taunted. "I scarcely felt a thing." His throat contracted in a painful spasm at the lie. In truth, Payter's powerful blow left a fiery ache in his side, and he found himself gasping for breath.

With an incoherent cry of rage, Payter fell upon him. The next blow caught him in center of the chest, and he staggered back a step before his captors jerked him forward. Digan fell to one knee, scraping the hide from his leg as the fabric of his leggings shredded on the sharp stones. He was forced upright again, with another hard shove to the middle of his back. He felt as if his arms would be wrenched from their sockets with all the pushing and pulling.

Payter's next blow caught Digan a glancing clip in the temple, and pain exploded from the side of his face. "Not so pretty now, are you, bard?" chortled a low voice in Digan's ear, and he felt a warm glob of spittle slide down his cheek. He twisted like an eel, but his arms were too tightly pinned. He could not free himself.

Payter waded in once more, dealing blows so thick and fast now that Digan couldn't have defended himself even if he were able to. When the smaller boy finally danced back with a triumphant grin, Digan hung motionless between his two captors. Only their unyielding grasp on his upper arms held him upright.

Marshaling every ounce of will left to him, Digan raised his head slowly to flash Payter a winsome smile through battered lips. "Do you feel all better now, little man?" he inquired, his voice honey sweet.

Payter's fist flashed out one final time, snapping the older boy's head to the side and plummeting Digan into darkness.

When he regained his senses, Digan lay crumpled

by the side of the road. His jaw ached unbearably, and he spat a broken tooth into the palm of his hand.

The only consolation is that Payter most likely fractured several fingers in order to inflict this much damage.

Wincing at the effort, Mordigan staggered to unsteady feet. The fire in his ribs was sharper now.

I hope it will not cause me greater trouble further down the road.

His right eye was swollen shut and the left little better. He explored his face with careful fingertips. There were abrasions from the skid along the rough stones down one cheek, and his upper lip was split, the cut still oozing blood as he swiped at it with the back of his hand.

What a pretty picture I must present right now, he thought wryly. *I, always so vain... I wonder what Allysian would say if she could see me now.*

The thought made his hand stray to his belt pouch as he limped down the road, and—though he was relieved to find his silver intact—his heart sank when he realized what was missing. He stumbled back to the scene of the fight, falling to his knees on the roadbed and searching the bloodstained ground for the comb.

I know it is a vain search, but I cannot leave without at least trying to find it. True, I wasn't intending to keep the thing...but it was hers, and it was oddly comforting to know it was there.

Anger smoldered to life beneath the pain as he beat the sides of his fists against the ground in frustration. *I will get Payter for this theft if it is the last thing I do! Not that I am likely to get the chance, now am*

I? Banished from the Hall and adrift on the road, there will be little reason for me to encounter the lout again.

Squinting to see from his left eye, Digan moved grimly on down the road for some distance, registering little of his surroundings until he found a watering trough standing before the tumbledown remains of a tiny cottage. As he stood in the dirt dooryard, he frowned. Something about the place stirred a vague sense of familiarity.

The homestead appeared to be abandoned, but there were a few inches of stagnant rainwater in the bottom of the trough. Gingerly, Digan dropped to one knee and sponged the worst of the blood from his face with the edge of his cloak. He examined his murky reflection critically. Both eyes were already blackening, and the cleaved lip would likely scar. The abraded cheek was nothing serious, but it added to his overall disreputable appearance.

Catching sight of a knuckle scraped in his confrontation with Payter earlier in the day, Digan gulped. "Thank you for your mercy, Lady Hathor," he whispered, profoundly grateful he was unable to fight back during the attack. *It was the mark of the rankest fool to risk my hands, and my future, so needlessly by brawling in the street.*

At least Payter did not think to damage my hands. If I could no longer play my instruments, it would not matter whether or not Master Cormeyer reconsidered his punishment.

"Thank heaven Payter is not very intelligent," Digan breathed aloud. "A creative attacker would have made sure to crush my fingers and destroy the very things that are a bard's essential tools." The mere thought of such a fate sent a wave of dizziness surging over him, and he hung his head between his knees until it passed.

Whatever else that beating did, it confirmed the fact nothing remains for me in town. Whatever Allysian's protests to the contrary, I am despised by practically everyone I know, and now even Master Cormeyer belongs among the throng...

There is nothing left to lose. I might as well do as Freitanya challenged—seek out Talthos and ask the wizard to make me a magical lute. Perhaps if I can gain such a prize alone, Master Cormeyer will see that I am no wastrel and grant me the papers I worked so hard to earn, and so desperately need.

Rising stiffly to his feet, Digan walked away from the town that held the only real home he'd ever known without even a backward glance. Digan never looked back.

Before long, the resiliency of youth reasserted itself, and the adventure of the moment seized Digan firmly in its grasp. The world lay ahead, and it was his to claim. Despite the pain, he hurried onward, eager to see what waited beyond the horizon.

The theft of Allysian's comb from his pouch was forgotten as Digan's thoughts turned to the future. He would live to regret the oversight.

CHAPTER 2

ALLYSIAN DIDN'T EVEN BOTHER to change her dusty gown. With her hair hanging in bedraggled tangles about her ears, and her dainty satin slippers ruined by the sharp stones of the road, she ran into the castle. Skirts hiked to her knees, she pelted through the broad corridors, barely registering the fine tapestries covering the stone walls, or the smudged chalk footprints she left on the thick carpeting. She ran straight to her father's throne room.

"Good heavens, girl," King Vasileios chided with an indulgent laugh, as she curtseyed before the dais supporting his gilt throne. "You look like something the cat has been playing with. Go and clean yourself up."

Fighting to catch her breath, she gasped out, "This can't wait, Father. You must intercede with Master Cormeyer. He has sent Mordigan Bryre away!"

The king frowned. "Really? That is strange. I thought the boy was his pride and joy. What on earth did the lad do now?"

"He was late for my lesson, and he had charge of the master's lute—but that was hardly enough to merit dismissal, Father!" She hurried up the steps to place an earnest hand on the padded velvet arm of his throne. "You have to do something."

"It is Master Cormeyer's decision to make, daughter," King Vasileios replied, giving her hand a gentle pat. "Now, go and change. You look like a ragamuffin."

"But, Father!"

"I will hear no more about it, Allysian." The king's brow knit once more into a frown, and the gray of his eyes darkened to steel.

He'll never listen when he is in this mood. I could just as soon persuade the frost to spare the roses.

Allysian gave up.

It is obvious that I will get no help in this matter. If I want to get Mordigan back in my life, she will have to do it myself. "Yes, Father," she answered, her eyes downcast, and her tone meek. "I'll go and change now."

Turning on her heel, Allysian hastened through the castle to her own chambers. The broad corridors continued, lit by filigree lamps hung from golden sconces. Fine wooden tables, polished like satin, held large bowls of fragrant blossoms the garden staff renewed daily. She plucked a blossom from a bowl in passing, holding it to her nose and breathing in its perfume with absent pleasure as her thoughts raced ahead of her flying feet.

She remembered a thousand fragments: memories of Mordigan that bloomed inside her head with more brilliance than the flowers lining the hallways.

Like the day that I was seven and tripped over the bottom step of the throne room dais, cutting my chin on the edge of the marble. Her fingers strayed to the tiny scar on the underside of her chin. *Digan held one sleeve to the wound to staunch the blood and wiped away my tears with the other, whispering silly doggerel until I laughed aloud and forgot what I had been crying about.*

Or the time when I was nine and my poor kitten climbed too high in the elm tree beside the palace gate. His face was as pale as Dame Madeline's sheets with worry as he went up the tree, but Digan climbed right up after it and brought it safely down tucked inside his shirt. I saw the claw marks he tried to hide from me.

Every time I needed protection or comfort, Digan was there. Well, now it is time for me to return the favor.

Now that she had made her decision, she felt a tingle of excitement that brought nervous giggles bubbling to her lips. *I will put things right. I will go and bring Digan home. And I will do it all by myself!*

It was a beautiful day, a pleasant breeze making the afternoon air cool for summer after the heat of the morning, but with a warm golden light that should last well into evening. The beckoning road smelled of baked earth and adventure. The caressing breeze carried a scent of growing wheat and promise. The pain in Digan's bruised side lessened as he walked, the stiffness gradually working itself out with exercise. He hooked thumbs through belt as he went along, humming his new song under his breath as he took stock of his resources.

The song was his lifeline. It tied him to his past, and held his hopes for the future. It comforted him and helped him sift through his thoughts. The soft humming was the only sound breaking the silence of the day.

This isn't so bad. I'm young and strong. A quick study. Surely there is something I can do with myself if Talthos will not heed my petition. But why should he not? If he wants payment, I can trade labor for the lute. I am willing to work.

The dust of the road puffed up around his boots as he walked, and he watched the play of the sunlight on the drifting motes. Despite his aches and pains, he was relatively content. His gaze wandered about him, taking in the smoothly cultivated fields, and the herd of cattle grazing in the far distance. The road was deserted as far as he could see, and he reveled in the solitude. Mordigan Bryre had always been a solitary boy, even in the midst of the bustling Guild Hall, so he was not afraid of being alone.

For the first time in his life, he had no responsibilities— no lessons to learn, or fingerings to practice. Even his recorder was hanging still on its peg in his room. Aside from his clothes—his second-best velvet and silk in honor of the princess' lesson, now bloodied and torn from the altercation—and the handful of silver Cormeyer bestowed upon him, all that he owned was his wits.

"And is that such a bad thing?" he said aloud, heartened by the sound of his own voice. "I may go where I please, and do as I like. 'Tis a fine life. I wager there is many a boy would give his arm for that freedom. Perhaps that is recompense enough. Why, I shan't miss the Hall one little bit." The bravado that was more than a little untrue grabbed his throat and squeezed. *Well, maybe I should keep such thoughts to myself,* he reasoned.

As for the task Freitanya proposed me...why not? I might as well seek out Talthos as anything else that comes to mind. But where should I start? The witch told me that the wizard lived "above the clouds" in his azure castle.

"On a mountaintop perhaps?" Digan mused, his brow puckered in a thoughtful frown. "There are no mountains here in Marineaux—and the witch did say that Talthos abandoned the realm—but there are large ranges on the borders with Nausa and Gwenthed both. Though I don't think there are any along the seacoast." He was beginning to get a little dizzy at the simple thought of searching the entire perimeter of the country on foot. "Hathor's Harp! There are mountains on the islands of Gondalyn and Suranaka too. Talthos could be almost anywhere!" The last words were almost a groan as he fully realized the magnitude of the task he set himself. *And to search out a wizard of Talthos' caliber unannounced...*

Talthos...even the name conjured up a vague tingle of foreboding that ran a shivering finger down Digan's spine.

I wonder what made him turn away from the kingdom? They say Talthos was the most powerful wizard of the age, before I was even born. Sult says that ever lived, but Garad and Roelf say Velachaz of Suranaka is stronger.

Digan found himself lecturing in his head. It was an old habit, fostered by a solitary personality. He scooped up a handful of pebbles from the road, and amused himself by juggling them as he walked, continuing the discourse as if trying to convince someone unseen of his facts.

His magic is legendary, and his skill as a musician made even Master Cormeyer jealous...but something happened about the time I was born, and I can't find anyone to tell me what. Talthos turned his back on

Marineaux and disappeared. The rumors say he is dead, but according to Freitanya, those reports are false.

The crone promised him a signpost. All he could do was wait until he found it.

Digan shrugged, dropping the stones and dusting his hands.

It is not a matter of urgency yet. I will see a bit of the country first. I've never been beyond the next town, and then only under the Master's watchful eye.

By the end of the day, however, the novelty of his adventure was beginning to wear thin. His soft boots were not intended for heavy wear, and his muscles were not used to the rugged exercise. On top of everything else, his ribs were beginning to ache again, and a bruise the size of a small plate mottled his side.

As the light began to fade from the sky, Digan found himself in the middle of open country with no sign of habitation in sight. The flat fields were no longer intriguing, but instead rather ominous when he began to contemplate the possibility of sleeping under the stars. "You've really gone and done it to yourself this time, Mordigan Bryre," he scolded aloud. "What kind of a fool are you? Getting yourself kicked out of a warm bed and a fine place just when you were finally going to amount to something. Now, you've ruined that for good and all. Just like you've ruined every other decent thing in your life with your lies and laziness."

I see there isn't even the slightest twinge of pain for that reproach. It is all too true.

Footsore and bone-weary, the boy trudged on until it became too dark to see even the white chalk road. A stand of trees loomed up to his right, a few hundred feet from the road, and he made for their shelter. The field between the roadway and the grove proved less level than it looked, and he stumbled when his foot hit a rabbit hole, twisting his ankle and falling headlong. He came down hard on his bad side, and gasped at the resulting wave of pain.

What am I doing here? How did it come to this?

Gritting his teeth, he got to his feet and limped into the scant refuge provided by the trees. Through blind luck, or celestial pity, he found a huge, hollow oak, and crawled inside. "Thank you, Lady Hathor," he whispered gratefully to his goddess.

Digan curled up in the shelter for the night, wrapping his thin cloak around him tightly—more for comfort than from cold. His stomach growled complaints at him, but he ignored it as best he could.

Whoever owns the fine fields I walked past this afternoon must be wealthy indeed, because their homesteads were not even visible from the road. It gave no opportunity to buy food, and I know nothing of foraging—beyond filching sweetmeats in the marketplace...

He resigned himself to a long, supperless night.

Mordigan Bryre lay with his fingers laced behind his head for some time, staring up at the stars spangling the velvet sky outside his shelter. He replayed the entire day in his head, trying to find some sense in it.

What would I do differently if given the chance? Would I still pick the fight with Payter? Would I strike the bargain with the witch? Would I tell Allysian—no, not even to myself may I let my thoughts stray there. She is a princess.

Digan was feeling more than a little bit sorry for himself by the time he finally drifted off to sleep. In one day, he went from being a pampered apprentice with a promising future to being a homeless wanderer with no appreciable skills and little means of supporting himself, and there was no one to blame but himself. It was not an auspicious turn of events.

Allysian surveyed the tiny bedchamber built into the storage bay of the Guild Hall with mingled curiosity and pity.

I know I shouldn't be here, but I wanted to see for myself...what exactly, I'm not sure.

Her heart was beating a ragged tattoo in her chest, and she stole nervous glances back over her shoulder toward the doorway. She left it ajar so she could hear if anyone approached but her blood pounded so loudly in her ears she doubted it would do much good.

For the bribe of a handful of sweets, Cormeyer's page let her inside, and now she stood in Digan's cubicle at the Guild Hall. Just large enough to hold the narrow bed and a simple clothes chest, the room was merely six feet of space partitioned off from one of the storage areas between the two floors of the hall. However, it was a sign of his former favored status that Digan owned these private quarters at all when all the other apprentices were in the common dormitory on the far side of the building.

How could Cormeyer so easily dismiss him, impossible as Digan could sometimes be? Papa is right. Digan was always the Master's pride and joy... This room only proves it. But where is Digan in this room? It is so bare and cold.

49

Aside from the furniture, the room held only a worn recorder hanging from a peg on the wall. There was no other imprint of Mordigan's personality.

Allysian knelt beside the clothes chest. It was a plain wooden box, bound with strips of bright brass, and she caught her bottom lip between her teeth as a sudden mental picture of Digan polishing the shining metal popped into her thoughts. She ran her finger along the band. *He is always so conscious of appearances. Who else would have worn velvet on a hot day like today?*

The princess opened the clothes chest, and a wave of aromatic scents wafted over her. There was the sharp, clean odor of the cedar wood itself, favored by cabinetmakers and joiners for precisely this property. Underneath the woody smell was the sweet aroma of freshening herbs that she recognized from her own wardrobes.

Another affectation of the fastidious Master Bryre...few of his fellow apprentices, and a good many of the masters, come to that, would know what the herbs are, much less use them amidst their clothing. She smiled, heart skipping a painful beat. *Whenever I think I understand him, he surprises me with a new facet of his personality.*

Stealing another look toward the doorway, well aware of the time she was wasting, Allysian lifted out a fine black velvet tunic, running her hand over the soft fabric like she was petting a cat.

I remember him wearing it to perform before the court last winter, regal as a young prince himself. His voice soared like a divine spirit, and I pretended he was singing only to me...

Shaking her head in irritation at her own foolishness, she laid the tunic aside with one final caress. Beneath its sable folds were more practical garments of forest green linen and black homespun. A broad smile of satisfaction bloomed across her face. *These are more like what I hoped to find.*

Allysian set the plainer clothes on the floor beside her and moved to replace the velvet tunic in the chest. As she did so, she caught a glimpse of something tucked carefully into the back corner of the box. Curious, she tugged it loose. What she held in her hand rocked her onto her heels in surprise.

"Why, Mordigan Bryre," she murmured, her voice a mere whisper of sound, "perhaps there is hope after all..."

The crumpled bit of ribbon was sky-blue satin, embroidered with tiny stars worked in threads of gold. She lost the bow years ago at her tenth birthday party...

She was in a fever pitch of excitement for weeks before the day, knowing that her father planned a very special celebration for the evening. There would be a puppet show, and jugglers, and best of all, Digan would sing. She did not get to see the boy as often as when they were younger, and such an occasion was a rare treat indeed.

The party was one brilliant spectacle after another, with glittering jewels reflecting the light of a thousand candles. The perfumed wax sent clouds of sweet-smelling smoke to collect around the stone vault of the ceiling. She was giddy with excitement, engrossed in a game of blindman's bluff with some of the gentry's children her father invited for the festivities.

Spinning after an elusive playmate, her eyes covered

with a silken cloth, she tripped, and started to fall, only
to be steadied and set upon her feet again. Tugging away
the blindfold, she found herself standing before Digan,
who looked decidedly uncomfortable to be there.

"It is high time you arrived, Mordigan Bryre," she
declared, with an imperious sniff. "You have kept me
waiting."

"I am sorry, Your Highness," he replied, executing a
stiff bow, "I was unavoidably detained."

"Hmph. Well, now that you are come at last, you must
sing at once." She spun on her heel and minced to her
throne, all haughty dignity, pretending that the moment
was unimportant to her. Seating herself on the miniature
version of her father's gilded chair, she commanded him
again, "Sing for me, Mordigan Bryre."

And sing he did...more beautifully than the
nightingales outside her window. The entire chamber
was silent in awe of it...

What prompted him to take away the hair ribbon?
How did he get hold of it...and why save it all this
time? Could it be?

Carefully Allysian replaced the keepsake in the bottom of
the box and resettled the velvet tunic. She gathered the plain
garments into her arms and rose to her feet. On impulse, she
lifted the recorder off its peg and added it to her bundle.

If I felt any second thoughts about my scheme, the
sight of that crumpled ribbon swept them away. I will
find Digan and bring him home.

Before she could step out onto the platform of the
storage bay, Allysian heard the creak of heavy steps
on the stairway and ducked back into the room, her
heart pounding so hard in her throat she thought

she would choke. She glanced frantically around the barren chamber, but there was nowhere to hide.

The door swung inward with a grating protest and she flattened herself against the wall behind it, one hand clapped across her mouth, and the other cradling her bundle to her chest. The panel screened her from view as long as the newcomer didn't close it behind him, and she held her breath.

What will I say if they catch me in here? That I was looking for Digan? No, Master Cormeyer knows better... By the Seven, don't close the door!

The door stayed open, and Allysian heard a deep, ragged sigh. A whiff of pipe smoke tickled her nostrils, and she raised her hand to press under her nose, praying not to sneeze.

"Digan, Digan...what will become of you now, my boy?"

Allysian peeked through the crack between the door and the jamb. Master Cormeyer stood in the doorway; one hand on the handle of the door, shoulders slumped. Deep furrows were carved in the crags of his face. He looked older than during her lesson even scant hours ago.

Papa was right, Allysian realized with a start. *Digan is Cormeyer's pride and joy. It must have hurt him terribly to send Digan away. It wasn't the act of injustice I thought, but a painful truth that must at last be faced: Digan is not meant to be a bard.*

But it is Digan's life. It is all he ever wanted in life... there must be some way to change Cormeyer's mind. If Digan would only come back and tell the Master the truth, I am sure Cormeyer would listen.

She would just have to go get the boy and bring him home at once.

Cormeyer sighed again, shaking his head as he pulled the door to behind him. Allysian put her ear to the thick panel, straining to hear whether his steps retreated down the stairs or went further into the storage bay. She wasn't sure, but time was wasting, and she decided at last that she must chance it.

I did, after all, run out of the Hall this afternoon without my lute. If I am caught downstairs, I will say that I came to fetch it. As for my bundle, well I will worry about that when the time comes.

Easing the door open, Allysian stepped out onto the landing. She tiptoed to the edge of the platform and peered over the edge. The hallway below her was empty, and the great door stood open to the sunlight. Lifting her skirts out of her way, she stole down the steps and out of the Hall.

Once she cleared the courtyard, she allowed herself the luxury of a moment's reaction, leaning against the outer wall and hugging Digan's clothing to her. She felt great shudders roll through her when she thought how close she came to being discovered. "You had better be worth it, Mordigan Bryre," she whispered aloud.

Making her way back to the castle, she slipped in through the main hall, and started for the stair.

"Where were you, little one?"

The quiet question startled her, and she whirled, hiding her bundle behind her.

Dame Madeline had been her nurse before becoming her governess— the closest thing she knew to a mother.

Allysian sketched a curtsey. "I— I was visiting in the village."

Madeline tsked. "Your father gives you too much freedom. You are a princess, Allysian, not a village hoyden. Look at you! And what is that you are hiding behind your back?"

"N-nothing. I promised to do a bit of mending for one of the stable boys." The lie sprang from her lips as smoothly as one of Digan's.

"What as I do to with you, child? Will you never learn your place?"

Allysian felt the blood rising hot in her cheeks. "Not if it means a kindness is beneath me," she answered tightly. "Now, if you will excuse me?" She turned and swept up the stair, ignoring Madeline's sharp call behind her.

Why must I be a princess? All I want is to be Allysian...and Digan. I want Digan by my side.

She made it to her bedchamber without further incident, more determined than ever to follow her heart. Standing in the luxurious dressing room, Allysian drew on Digan's clothes, breathing deeply of the herbs that perfumed them. The scent brought a lump to her throat.

I caught that same slightly flowery smell under the sharper scent of sweat as I hugged Digan on the road earlier...

The thought of that embrace sent a wave of heat rushing into her cheeks, and yet her biggest regret was that she had lacked the nerve to kiss him too.

She bit her lip. *What am I thinking of? I can't believe how brazen I'm becoming!*

The clothes were much too large for her, the sleeves of the tunic falling to her fingertips. She rolled them up to her elbows, and moved toward her wardrobe for some kind of sash, one hand clutching the breeches about her middle. She riffled through the cabinet until she found a plain leather belt she sometimes wore when hunting with her father, and cinched it tight around her slim waist. Pulling on a pair of soft boots sweet-talked from one of the palace stable boys, she looped the recorder over her shoulder to rest against her hip.

Glancing at her reflection in the polished brass mirror, Allysian caught her breath with a gasp.

How could I have forgotten?

She swept up her sewing scissors and took a deep breath. Her hair hung in golden waves to well below her waist. Taking a large hank in one hand, she sawed it off roughly at her chin and tossed the strands to the floor at her feet. It became easier after the first cut was made, and soon she stood in a heap of spun gold.

She studied her reflection once more, turning her head this way and that as she marveled at how light it felt. *Without all the great weight of hair pulling it down, it feels as if my head will float off.*

She giggled at the notion.

"That is a habit you must break, my girl—lad," she lectured her reflection with a stern frown. *"No self-respecting boy your age would giggle like a ninny."* She fluffed the ragged ends of her hair with one hand, shivering a little from the feel of air against her neck.

The cut isn't very even, but it will have to do.

Allysian refastened her belt outside her tunic and

bloused it out above her waist. She scowled at the resulting reflection with a dubious frown. Her features weren't what one would call "pretty" in a classic sense, but more boyish, and her figure had more angles than curves.

Maybe I will be able to manage the deception—if no one looks too closely...

Allysian shrugged. *There is no time to ponder the matter further. Digan already has quite a head start on me, and I will be stopped if I don't go now while everyone is busy preparing the evening meal.*

She left the chamber without another thought, ignoring the tangled pile of gold on the stone floor.

When Digan awoke the next morning, he suffered a moment's disorientation as to how the walls of his room had crept inward until he remembered where he was and why. The ancient tree smelled of decayed wood and damp leaves, and there were bits of moldy bark in his hair. He raked fingers through the tangled strands with a grimace of distaste. His hand ran across something slimy, and he yanked it out of his hair with a startled cry. Glancing down, he flung the fat slug into the field outside his tree.

Resting head on bent knees, he gave in to a moment's despair. *How am I going to survive in the world? Great Hathor, I ruined my life for good this time.*

The gray light of pre-dawn filtered through the opening of the great oak, and Digan sighed. There is no point in putting things off. Day always began with the sun at the Hall, and I can see no reason to alter that routine.

He scrambled out of the tree on his hands and knees, and levered himself to his feet, groaning over twinges from muscles he never knew existed. His body ached all over. The injuries sustained in Payter's beating had stiffened overnight, and the walking done the previous day had also taken its toll.

Hungry, sore, and mouth parched from thirst, Digan returned to the deserted road, and began to limp on in the direction he was traveling the day before. He knew not where the road would take him, but it was far away from the Hall, and that was enough for the moment.

A vista of cultivated fields surrounded him on both sides of the roadway, but he still saw no signs of habitation. "Not that I can see much of anything at present," he said aloud, comforted by the sound of his own voice as he scanned the countryside through his slitted left eye. The right was still swollen completely shut. "Ah well, probably for the best. I doubt I present a very good case for charitable hospitality. Not if I look half as bad as I feel."

The renewed exercise soon began to work out the kinks in his muscles, but it only aggravated his other problems. His stomach began to provide a steady commentary on his sad state of affairs, and he remembered with longing the musical fountain in the town square. The gleaming white stone of the buildings; the polished marble of the basin with its ceaselessly tumbling spray; the lounging boys with homespun and silk—depending on their rank in the unofficial hierarchy of the square—it all seemed a dream.

Was it truly only yesterday morning that I stood on the sandstone flags and knocked Payter down for insolence?

This lonely beckoning roadway was the only thing that held any reality to him in the growing light of his first full day of exile.

Going a day, or even two, without food or water won't kill me—I've done it often enough before—but this time there will be no hearty meal waiting when the punishment is over.

He wracked his brains to remember how far it was to the next town or village, but there was only a vague impression of several hours spent in the back of a plodding cart.

Even so, the draft animals put your limping progress to shame, jeered the voice inside his head.

"At least I didn't break my ankle in that hole," he reminded himself in a stern tone. "It might be much worse."

Or a damn sight better, his subconscious replied, the ghost of a pain teasing his throat as he tried to lie to himself.

The thirst is the most annoying thing. He kept watch along the side of the road for a spring or pond, but not even a puddle presented itself. *I would settle for the brackish water from the bottom of that trough.*

Remembering a trick Master Cormeyer taught him in order to improve his diction—and how it always made his mouth water—he found a round white pebble and popped it under his tongue. It helped to trick his mind into thinking he no longer thirsted, and now that his biggest problem was solved, he could indulge his curiosity.

While the area immediately outside the town was flat, and mostly under cultivation, here the broad chalky road wound through increasingly wilder countryside. The endless fields were disappearing, and he could see stands of trees curving away on either side of the roadway.

As the morning wore on, ranks of tumbled clouds began to build in the sky, and Digan kept an uneasy eye on the horizon. Rain would make his travel even more miserable...

The summer heat pressed down in palpable waves. Imprisoned in the rags of his velvet doublet, Digan mopped the sweat from his brow with his ragged sleeve. He contemplated removing the garment, but his pride still forebear it.

Humping swells rimmed the road, where the land was beginning to rise towards foothills that would grow to mountains over the border. The grass on the verges of the road was thick and green, but just beginning to yellow as the summer passed its halfway point. When the fall harvest arrived, the owners of the small farms and tenant peasants would cut it for winter feed, but at present, it provided a restful distraction as he walked. The breeze cut patterns in the waving stalks that constantly shifted and reformed as he watched. Its wayward breath eased the heat a little, and lifted Digan's heart.

By the time the sun climbed to noon, however, no amount of distraction could take his mind off his growling stomach. His last meal was a snatched biscuit in the dining hall yesterday at dawn.

Just as the sun reached its zenith, he spied a lazy curl of smoke rising from the chimney of a small cabin nestled snugly in the wooded skirts of the road. The friendly breeze brought a tantalizing whiff of something wonderful, and he followed his nose to the source of the fragrance. Digan could smell fresh bread baking, and a savory aroma that promised heartier fare.

Cutting through the knee-high grass to the dirt dooryard of the tiny dwelling, he rapped tentatively on the wooden panel. It opened a crack, and he saw a bright button eye.

"What?" asked a suspicious female voice.

"Fowgif mwe—" Digan hurriedly spat the pebble into his hand, whipped his dusty green cap off his head, and began again. "Forgive me, mistress," he said, in his best bard's purr, "but I have walked many miles this day, and I wondered if you might spare a crust of that new baked bread. I'm willing to work for it—" he added hastily.

"Hmph," the woman sniffed. "And what does a beggar in silk and velvet know of work? Mayhap you got those bruises from a dissatisfied employer—or was it a potential victim who caught you before you could complete your theft?"

Digan flushed. It stung his pride to the quick to be named beggar and thief—but his empty stomach was more than willing to overlook the slight...and let it be known...loudly.

"Well, I suppose it would do no one good to have you starve to death on my doorstep," the woman grumbled. "Come inside."

"Thank you, my lady," murmured Mordigan, with his deepest court bow.

The woman tittered like a serving wench, and stepped back from the doorway to let him enter.

The inside of the little house was spare and neat, reminding him of Cormeyer's personal quarters at the Music Hall—a day and night contrast to the cluttered office.

His hostess was a tall, buxom woman with soft, brown hair pulled back in a neat bun, red highlights shimmering in the sleek waves. Her sparkling brown eyes were wide set in her tan face, and the crows-feet in their corners bespoke of frequent laughter. She wiped strong hands on her apron and gestured to the table.

"Have a seat, young sir. You look like you could use a bit of rest. I'll fetch you a bowl of my soup and a slice of that bread. What are you doing so far from home? For you are not from hereabouts, that much I know."

"I seek my fortune, lady," he replied with an airy wave of his hand. "Destiny called to me, and I answered it."

"Pretty words. What do they mean?"

Digan frowned. "I don't understand your question..."

"What do you seek as 'fortune', boy? What 'destiny' had time to dicker with you personally? Was it the one who disliked your pretty face so violently?"

"I—" Again he was pulled up short by his promise to Freitanya. *I cannot reveal my quest, and I cannot lie.*

"I was dismissed from my place," he said at last staring at the work-polished grain of the tabletop with a sullen scowl. "I have nowhere special to go. As for the beating, lady—I assure you, I did nothing to deserve it." The last statement contained more than a touch of falsehood, and he paid for it, coughing as a sudden painful contraction tightened his throat.

"I've just the thing for that cough," commented the woman, moving to the cupboard and pulling out various odds and ends. "It will fix you right up," she promised, stirring a bit of this and a pinch of something else into a mug of water. "Here, boy. Drink this."

Digan took the cup and examined it with a dubious frown. He sniffed the liquid. It smelled of herbs and sunlight. *What could it hurt?*

He took a tentative swallow. The concoction ran smoothly down his aching throat, and left a pleasant aftertaste of precious honey and something lemony... but there were hints of other ingredients he didn't recognize at all. It took away the last dregs of the pain in his throat, however, and seemed to soothe his other aches as well.

"Thank you, my lady," he murmured with sincere gratitude as she set down a platter heaped with bread and a large wooden bowl of soup.

"Eat hearty, boy. You could use some fattening."

Digan was more than willing to oblige. The food was plain but tasty, and he soon cleaned the dishes. "It was a splendid meal."

"You looked as if you needed it," she replied as she whisked the dishes into and out of the rinse bucket. "Lord knows, it was little enough." She plopped down on the bench opposite him and fixed him with a level stare. "What has set you wandering upon the road, Mordigan Bryre?"

Digan started back. *I know I never mentioned my name. How does this woodcutter's wife know of me?*

"I-I do not understand, lady...as I say, I lost my place—"

"And there was no other to be had in the whole town? It is most unpopular you must be."

Something about the tone of her voice made a ripple of fearful recognition shiver up his spine, but it was gone before he could grasp hold of it. "I fear 'Tis true, my lady," he affirmed ruefully, "I'm not the best beloved youth in the town. There will be more people glad to see the back of me than sorry."

"A sad state of affairs for one so young." She rose from the table and busied herself about the kitchen. "No skills, no education...whatever shall you do with yourself, Digan?"

He was beyond being uneasy to being frightened. *How does she know so much about me? I am not quite so vain as to believe my history is common knowledge throughout the countryside.*

He made a sign against evil under the table, and leapt to his feet. "P-perhaps I should be going—"

"And what about my payment? You promised me work for my food."

Digan fumbled in his belt pouch and held out the silver coins in a trembling hand. "H-here. I will pay for it."

"Foolish boy. Not everything can be bought. I have no need of your silver. On the other hand, I could use a strong back and another pair of hands in the field this afternoon. Help me with the weeding, and we will call it even."

Digan wanted to put as much space between him and the woman as possible as soon as he could. *But it would be rude to deny her request when I made the offer—and if she is the seer she appears to be—it might be dangerous as well.*

"As you desire, my lady," he replied meekly.

By the end of the afternoon, he was beginning to wish he had taken his chances with flight. He lost sight of the woodcutter's wife as he tolled in one section of the field, and she in another. It made the work both easier and more tedious to bend over the rows alone.

Only strength of will kept him moving by the end of the day. His fingers, while bearing thick calluses gained from long hours of plucking the strings of his lute, were unaccustomed to other work, and they were blistered and bleeding before the sun set. His battered ribs ached like dull coals, and his back was strained from bending to pull the weeds. To top everything off, his tunic was torn in three more places.

He examined the rents in the black velvet with a mournful eye. *This is my favorite suit of clothing, well cut and flattering in fit. It took me half a year to earn its price. Now it looks like beggar's finery indeed.*

Digan sighed. *What am I doing here? If I swallow my pride and beg Master Cormeyer to give me another chance, I feel sure he will relent. Maybe I should just go home.*

But the thought was only a fleeting one. Payter would have trumpeted the news of his defeat throughout the town. *I can never go crawling back. No, I cannot return without the lute that will prove my merit—at least to myself.*

"That's enough for today, boy," commanded the woman, coming up beside him with cat-like quiet, as she dusted her hands on her apron. "You more than paid for one meal. Come and eat some supper, and I'll give you a bed for the night. You can be on your way in the morning."

Digan nodded with a weary sigh of acceptance. It was sensible advice. Even the thought of trying to strike out tonight made him feel faint at heart. Wincing at a particularly fierce twinge of pain from his hands, he bit back the moan that rose to his lips.

"Let me take a look at those," the lady clucked, reaching for his hands with a gentle touch. He examined them along with her, running a critical gaze over the damage. His long fingers were torn and swollen, and the palms blistered and raw. "Poor boy," she scolded with a sympathetic cluck of her tongue. "'Tis a good thing you have no concert tonight. Why did you not say something? You near ruined your fine hands."

Digan shrugged. "What matter? I no longer have an instrument to play anyway. I suppose I should become used to working with my hands. I shall have to do something to earn my keep."

"Come inside, lad." The woman draped a comforting arm around his shoulders. "I'll tend to your blisters and give you something for the pain you are trying so stoically to deny. You mustn't keep everything hidden from the world. Even the bravest man sometimes knows fear and loneliness."

Digan wanted to pull away from her encircling arm, but found himself powerless to do so. A chill ran through him. *What have I gotten myself into?*

Allysian was also having second thoughts. Her first night was spent huddled in a miserable ball in the middle of an open field without even the slim comfort provided by Digan's light cloak. She left the village some hours behind the boy, and although she didn't know it, veered quite a bit off his course by mistaking the way at a fork in the road.

On the second day, while Digan worked for his meals at the woodcutter's cottage, Allysian plodded along the road towards the Nausean border, working herself into a fine state of temper. "What in the name of the Seven Virgins am I doing here? Chasing after a no-account, lying, cheating scoundrel like Mordigan Bryre when I could be home in my nice safe palace with my nice soft bed, and I wouldn't look like a bloody fool."

Hot tears of fury welled behind her eyes, and she screwed up her face and willed them be gone. "I cut my hair for you, Mordigan Bryre," she murmured into the empty afternoon, one hand straying to the ragged fringe about her neck. "Do you know how long it took to grow it? Do you care? No! Do you care about anything except yourself and your stubborn, stiff-necked pride? No! Damn you, Mordigan Bryre!"

She was no longer sure that the whole affair was worth the aggravation. "It's not as if he was ever nice to me anymore," she continued, her anger building. "After all, Digan hardly seems to know that I exist. A crumpled hair-ribbon in the bottom of some stupid chest doesn't constitute eternal worship." An awful thought struck her, and she froze in her tracks. "By the Circle, for all I know, he doesn't even remember it is there. He could have thrown it into that chest years ago and forgotten all about it!" *Just because I harbor some childish infatuation doesn't mean he feels the same towards me...*

And then the image of Digan's stricken face when Cormeyer dismissed him flashed through her memory. *There is no one else to care. He needs me.*

Allysian continued down the road. The sun was beginning to set on her first full day as a vagabond. It slipped toward the horizon in a blaze of golden splendor. She caught her breath at the sight of it. It was dazzling in its beauty. The sky was awash with scarlet and purple banners of cloud, embroidered with the gold thread of the last sunbeams.

I've never seen such a lovely sunset.

"Do you see it, Digan?" she whispered in awe. "Wherever you are, do you see it? Are you thinking of me?"

Her voice trailed away to wistful silence, and one of the tears she was reining in managed to slip her leash. She dashed it away with a sigh.

The sunset might be beautiful, but it means another lonely night is coming.

Allysian shuddered at the thought of another night alone in the fields, with every whisper of the wind sounding like approaching bandits, and every night bird like avenging ghosts.

"The night will be a cold one," commented a cracked voice.

Allysian whirled, every nerve in her body tingling, and her heart thundering with shock. A stooped form leaning on a crooked staff peered back at her intently. "G-good day, mistress," the princess murmured. Her manners instinctively came to her rescue. She curtseyed before she remembered her assumed disguise, and then stood in awkward dismay, not knowing how to extricate herself from the mistake.

"Prettily done, my dear," chuckled the crone, "but hardly the greeting one expects from a page boy."

Allysian bit her lip, berating herself soundly for making such a stupid error. *You must start thinking like a boy if you want to deceive anyone, you little fool.*

"It will get easier, Princess," promised the withered hag, and Allysian felt the hair on the back of her neck stand on end.

"H-how did...who?"

"You are not as well-schooled as your Digan in the ways of the world, are you, Allysian?" the woman tsked. "What do they teach you in your ivory tower? I am Freitanya!" She threw her arms skyward, and thunder cracked in the now cloudless heavens. "All who know of me fear my wrath!"

Allysian gulped. She was not so sheltered that the name was unknown to her. She took an involuntary step backward.

"Don't look so terrified, girl!" the witch continued in a milder tone, a merry twinkle in her dark eyes. "I gave up eating children years ago. 'Twas bad for my stomach."

The princess giggled in spite of her fright.

"That's better, my pretty," Freitanya cooed, patting Allysian's arm with a twisted, claw-like hand. "Now, come with me. We have much to discuss." She ambled off, crooking a finger at the girl over her shoulder.

Allysian ran to catch up. "Um...excuse me, mistress...but where are we going?"

Freitanya turned back to the girl, her eyes suddenly serious. "We are going to examine whether or not you truly desire what you seek, my child... because if you don't—you best return to Vasileios' pretty palace now, before two fragile hearts are needlessly shattered."

Allysian cocked her head and frowned. "If you mean do I 'truly desire' to help Mordigan Bryre, then the answer is yes. He needs me. He thinks that everyone in the world has abandoned him, and I won't let him keep on feeling that way. I won't!" The princess folded her arms across her chest defiantly, but her quivering chin gave her away. She was tired, hungry, and emotionally battered. There was little left for her to give, but what little there was belonged to Digan. She was more determined than ever to find him and bring him home.

"I believe you, my dear," murmured Freitanya in a voice like silver honey. She grew taller as her twisted limbs straightened, and her dark eyes seemed to eclipse the world. "There is steel in you, and softness as well. That young man is lucky to have you on his side...does he realize that?"

"I-I don't know," Allysian whispered, ducking her head. She felt the prick of the harnessed tears behind her lashes, and again willed them not to fall. She must be strong. She had to be...for Digan's sake. When she found him, it would take every bit of that strength to get him to return home.

Suddenly, she felt warm arms around her, and a soothing voice murmuring words of comfort. "We will save him, little one. From himself as well as from the world. But you must trust me."

Wordlessly, Allysian nodded. She walked with the witch into the last rays of the setting sun. The golden beams shimmered and danced about them...and the road lay bare among the lengthening shadows.

Digan collapsed onto a bundle of straw in the woodcutter's shed well before Allysian's sunset, and slept like the dead. He half expected the man would come home before nightfall, but the goodwife brushed aside his worries, stating that her husband was often afield for days and would never even know the boy was their guest. She bound his ribs tightly under a poultice, and given him a draught he suspected aided in his heavy sleep.

After a good night's rest, Digan felt better able to face his search for the Azure City. The pain in his side was relegated to a vague ache, and his right eye was actually usable this morning, if still a bit swollen.

"Thank you for the hospitality, my lady. I will never forget your kindness."

"Pretty words, young sir—but like as not you will forget an old woman like me the moment some dainty miss catches your eye."

"I would not lie to you, my lady," Digan protested. *I dare not...*he added to himself silently.

"Go on with you, rascal!" scoffed the woodcutter's wife, handing him a neat parcel of food for his journey. "Follow the road west into Nausa until you reach land's end, and you will find what you seek."

"But I—" began Digan, and then broke off in confusion. He had not told her what it was that he sought, but an uneasy suspicion told him that she knew anyway. "Thank you again for the food and shelter, lady." He gave her his finest bow, and started off in the direction she indicated.

Two days after that fateful meeting on the road

with Freitanya, Allysian was beginning to wish that she never listened to the witch's advice, even though she parted with the crone more determined than ever to rescue Digan from himself.

Freitanya counseled her to come to Nausa and wait for Mordigan Bryre to arrive. So far, however, there was no sign of the boy, and the princess could not believe that she was so far ahead of him. "He like as not turned aside and is halfway to Wyndwell by now," the girl grumbled to herself. "You have only the witch's word he was even heading in this direction, fool. He could have gone to sea and crossed to Suranaka by now!"

Allysian crouched behind the wheel of a market cart, studying the baker's wagon across the way with a covetous eye. Her hair hung in greasy straggles about her ears, and there was a wide streak of dirt across one sunburned cheek. There was little hint of the dainty princess in the grimy, bedraggled urchin contemplating the theft of a currant bun.

And Allysian was starving.

Nervously smoothing her tunic about her hips, she squared her shoulders and strolled casually across the open market square. With a slightly off-key whistle, she thrust thumbs into belt and sauntered past the baker's cart. As she drew even with the wagon, she snaked out a hand and snatched one of the buns.

"Hey! You there—" an angry voice shouted.

Clutching the bun, Allysian took to her heels, weaving through the stalls of the market. She heard the sound of pursuit behind her and increased her speed. Glancing back over her shoulder to gauge how closely she was being followed, she barreled into a hard but yielding surface, which knocked her to the ground.

Allysian looked up to find a huge figure in the uniform of a city guard glowering down at her. "Oops," she gulped.

*In for a penny...*she shrugged, cramming the bun in her mouth as the guardsman jerked her roughly to her feet. He shook her like a puppy, and then cuffed her hard across the face.

"You won't get away with a trick like that on my watch, my boy!" growled her captor.

Head whirling dizzily, Allysian was quietly— and thoroughly—sick. *Oh well,* she thought miserably, *I tried...*

The guardsman swore, dragging her behind him. "We'll just see what the court has to say about this."

Stumbling after the soldier, the princess tried to devise a plan of escape, but she couldn't think of a thing. *Perhaps I will be able to talk my way out of trouble before the magistrate. I can always wheedle Papa around to my point-of-view— he is firmly wrapped around my finger when it came to unimportant matters. Why, in the name of all that is holy, did he not intervene with Cormeyer and save me from this wretchedness?*

She drew her sleeve across her throbbing lip, and it came away bloody.

I certainly hope Mordigan Bryre appreciates all the trouble he has caused me—whenever he deigns to show himself.

Digan stared upward with a sinking heart. "Until you reach land's end" the woodcutter's wife said—

and here it was. The cliff towered above him, a forbidding rock face with slim hand and foot holds vaguely visible among the shadows.

It was his fourth day of travel, and he crossed the border into the neighboring kingdom of Nausa just at noon, and followed the sun until the road played out at the base of this mountain.

To go around it will take a day at least, and that passing farmer advised me there is only sea beyond it. The cliff must be the landmark of which the goodwife spoke...and the Azure City lies above it. There is nothing to be done but to climb the sheer stone.

With a shuddering breath, he set his boot onto the first foothold and started up. Digan moved slowly and carefully, testing each step before he committed his weight to it. The higher he rose, the harder it was to breathe.

It was not that the air was actually thinner, but it certainly seemed so. His battered hands were soon raw and bleeding from scrapes and nicks garnered among the sharp rocks.

Reaching for a hold that proved to be just beyond his grasp, his foot slipped, and Digan's scraped cheek slammed against the side of the mountain with bruising force before he caught himself, heart pounding in his chest. He clung spread-eagled and motionless for an infinite space of time, eyes squeezed shut as images of plunging to the jagged ground below played behind his lids.

CHAPTER 3

DIGAN MOANED LOW IN his throat like a wounded animal, eyes squeezed shut as he fought to regain control. Behind his closed lids, a vivid scene replayed in sharp detail.

"You can't to it, Digan! You're too little." The jeering voice of Portean, long since gone from the Hall, but senior apprentice on that long-ago day. *"Stay down there where it is safe."*

The sun beat down on the dusty courtyard, drawing perfume from the roses in a heady cloud. It was a half-holiday, lessons over for the day, and the boys left to mischief.

"I ain't scared," Digan replied hotly. He knew he was small for his age—his growth still in the future—and sensitive about that fact. He grabbed onto the ivy snaking up the rough wall of the Hall and began to climb.

It was a dare. Climb to the roof of the Hall and touch the flagstaff supporting the Guild pennant. It was a rite of passage for all the apprentices, and most attempted it at some point or other. But most were nine or ten before they tried. Digan was six.

He wouldn't be climbing now, but Portean and Laeran were teasing him about his size, and lack of family. He must prove them wrong. He was not too little. Not a homeless mongrel. He was a bard, and fearless as a lion. He would show them.

It was an easy climb at first, but as he reached the edge of the roof and started to swing onto the slates, he slipped, and fell backward. The sensation of helpless terror seemed to stretch forever. His heart thundered like a drum in his ears and then the ground slammed into his back and the world went black.

When he awoke, he was ensconced in the Master's bed, a bandage around his head, and his arm broken in two places. Cormeyer sat on the edge of the bed, shaking his head. "What am I to do with you, son?"

Well, now he knew...

Ever since the fall, Digan was deathly afraid of heights. It was another secret he hid behind his bravado and boasting, but the fear was a demon he could never completely shake. Only the thought of the wonders he would be able to perform with the magical lute—and how the instrument would redeem him in the eyes of Cormeyer—forced his leaden feet upward.

It was growing dark now, and a chill wind blew in these rocky heights that belied the summer season. The gusts grew stronger as Digan inched his way forward, ripping at his cloak and blowing his long hair into his eyes. He didn't dare loosen his grip to dash it away, so he endured the sting of the lashing strands as they whipped about his face. The rising wind carried the sharp scent of rain, and Digan shivered.

He fought his way upward with grim determination, not trusting himself to look beyond the bare stone immediately in front of him.

I can't turn back now. There is nowhere to go but up. Nowhere to rest. I must keep going...

The wind continued to rise, buffeting him with merciless gusts of power as he clung to the rock with the tenacity of a spider. It tore at him now, trying to wrench loose his fragile hold. Lightning began to dance among the rocks, the air sizzling around him, searing bolts whip-cracking on all sides as if toying with him. Digan inched upward with dogged resolution, step by painful step.

The chill rain promised by the wind began to pelt him, and the rocks turned to glass beneath his feet. His boots could find no purchase on their slick surfaces. For each step forward he won, he slipped back half, and the wind howled around him with manic glee.

The air smelled of ozone and the acrid sweat of fear beneath the sharp clarity of the rain. Digan was exhausted, as much from fighting through his terror as from the exertion of the climb. Each step was a battle won against his implacable foe, but his reserves were failing. Hot tears mixed unbidden with the cold rain. After trying so hard, and coming so far, the thought of failure was bitter indeed.

Will I die here on this barren cliff-side, unnoticed and unmourned?

Just when he felt he could go no further, his reaching hand closed on empty air. His bleary gaze fought to focus through the sodden curtain of hair obscuring his vision, and he spied a shallow hollow in the rock before him. Not deep enough to merit the name of niche, it merely offered a narrow ledge to rest upon through the misery of the downpour.

"Thank you again, Lady Hathor, you are too kind." He placed his back against the cliff face and huddled into a shivering ball, his drenched cloak pulled over his head to screen out the driving rain. He rested forehead on bent knees, trying not to feel sorry for himself. To do so did no good, and he despised the weakness it revealed.

I am too old for such self-indulgent nonsense. I brought this on myself, didn't I? It is all a result of my stubborn pride and my damnable lying.

He no longer remembered when the lying started, or why.

Perhaps jealousy over the families I so envied my friends prompted me to invent stories of my own past, or it may be shame that I could not read and write that made me boast of other attributes. Whatever the cause initially, the lies are second nature to me now. I spout them without thinking. That brief time spent with the woodcutter's wife quickly showed me how difficult it will be to avoid the effects of the witch's spell.

Wet and miserable, Digan stretched out as best he could on the narrow ledge, his back pressed tight against the rock of the niche and let himself drift into sleep. There was no point trying to move forward in the rain, particularly as the daylight was beginning to fade behind the steel gray of the clouds.

Tomorrow I will find the Azure City. If I survive the night...

Mordigan awoke to find himself in the center of a rose and gold cloud. Tendrils of vapor curled around him like inquisitive sprites as the dawn mist pressed closer. Disoriented, he started to crawl forward, and put his hand out into nothingness.

Digan fell back against the rock with a sharp cry. His heart pounded so hard he shook all over. He hugged himself tightly, rocking against the shudders until he could finally calm his skittering heartbeat. It was several terrified minutes before he could steel himself to move again.

By then, the vivid colors of the sunrise were faded to a uniform white blur as the clouds spread out around him. All he could see were billowing waves of cotton wool, and the harsh reality of the cliff at his back. The rock stretched on above him, melting into the fog a few feet beyond his reach. At least he could see that much. Beneath him, the world completely vanished.

Even if I wanted to turn back—and his newfound honesty admitted that the temptation presented itself—*I dare not risk the descent. There is nothing to be done but keep climbing, and hope that whatever I find at the end of this quest will eventually lead me home.*

Every inch upward was hard won as he compelled himself to go on. His hands trembled as they reached for the tiny projections and hollows that offered him their fragile holds, and his feet moved through sheer will alone.

When he reached the top of the cliff at last, Digan heaved himself onto the level ground, fingers digging grateful furrows in the soft turf until his muscles stopped twitching from nervous strain. He rolled upon his back, his eyes closed as he relished the sun on his upturned face and the solid earth beneath him.

I could do without rain for a while.

The warmth of the sunlight soaked deep into his aching limbs, and soothed him back into an exhausted slumber. He dreamt of Allysian, not as she was now, when he was all too painfully aware of their relative positions, but as she was as a child, when he was a frequent visitor to the castle.

In the dream, he was back at the birthday party where ten-year-old Allysian solemnly bade him kneel at her feet after performing for the guests, and presented him with the ribbon from her hair as a token of her favor. He was flushed with excitement from the performance, having poured his soul into the concert, and her hand was cool on his as she placed the ribbon into it.

She called him her "true bitter knight," having misheard the title of "troubadour," and earned admiring applause from the assembled court. It was a pretty gesture from the romantic child, but the twelve-year-old apprentice knew in his head that it was nothing more. Oh, but in his heart...

The bit of sky-blue ribbon was the only possession Digan truly regretted leaving behind. It was his dearest treasure. He sighed in his sleep, and sank beyond dreams. The relative chill of the lengthening shadows finally awakened him.

Digan sat up with a start, staring about him wildly. He found himself on the edge of a verdant green meadow which ended on one hand at the sharp cliff-face, and on the other rolled out of sight in gentle velvet swells of thick emerald grass studded with white, star-like flowers. Their scent rode the breeze, perfuming the afternoon with an indefinable fragrance hinting at roses and wood-smoke, but close kin to neither.

To his left, a stretch of road beckoned, curling away into the distance. Well rested, and eager to explore any way forward that did not entail climbing back down the cliff, Digan rose to his feet.

When he stood, the horizon became more distinct, and he gasped in wonder. Although still a league distant, he could see a shimmering city sparkling beneath the rays of the westering sun. Blue fire danced from facets reflecting back the light.

Somehow, it never occurred to me that the name "Azure City" was literal.

He started toward the glittering city, then hesitated, darting an uneasy glance over his shoulder at the cliff. Behind him was a sea of white mist, the tops of the clouds that made his morning climb so miserable. Even the brief thought of retracing his steps sent an expressive shudder rolling through him, and he continued walking toward the sapphire fire of the distant towers.

The road was nothing like the broad white thoroughfare he followed out of Marineaux. Its narrow track was half-obscured in places by tall grass and clumps of the little white flowers. Deep ruts scored it, but their edges were blunted and weathered, as if no traffic had traversed this once busy road in a very long time.

By the time he reached the towering gates, he realized his initial impression was misleading. It was not an actual city he approached, but a sprawling keep, with several outbuildings, and a high wall encircling the compound. The entire structure was a clear blue crystal, which glowed in the sunlight as if lit from within.

Digan could see vague shapes and patterns beneath the surface of the stone. *It's like I am looking through a frozen lake onto a drowned world...*

There were scaffolds against several of the walls, as if the builders but paused in their labors, but there was a thick layer of dust upon the walkways, and a desolate air to the enclosure, which suggested that the pause was a long one.

Digan stood before the closed gates, studying the intricate carvings that decorated the cerulean panels. The craftsmanship was exquisite, awe-inspiring in the delicate strength of its patterned carvings. The veins of gold delineating the tracery of leaves and vines bordering the lintel and jambs were worth a king's ransom. His hand crept forward of its own accord, finger tracing the grooves of the carving. The stone was cool and smooth as glass beneath his touch.

High banks of white roses grew all along the base of the wall, creating the impression that the castle thrust up out of a bed of clouds. They perfumed the air with their sweet scent, reminding him with an aching jolt of the roses outside the Master's window. Dark blue blossoms were scattered throughout the roses, and Digan bent to sniff the unusual blooms.

These blue flowers are like nothing I've ever seen before. Their scent is surprisingly pungent... unpleasant on its own, but when it blends with the roses, it creates something wonderful. Somehow, exotic...

Chewing his lip with pensive absent-mindedness, and wincing at the resultant pain, Digan wondered again if he were doing the right thing. The wizard was obviously rich and powerful as well as a high-ranking magic user.

Why should Talthos deign to aid a penniless apprentice who could not even keep his place? King Vasileios' father commissioned Master Cormeyer's lute for a large sum of gold. Whatever made me think the wizard would grant a homeless boy like me such a prize simply for the asking?

Digan thought of the crevasse yawning behind him, and a wave of dizziness washed over him. Hard as it was to force himself *up* that precipice, the idea of going back down it again was much worse. It would be far easier to endure the wizard's wrath.

And what do I have to lose? Even if the wizard strikes me down for my temerity, who will miss me?

A fleeting whisper of self-pity ran through him, but Digan forced it away.

What is done is done. My future is what I seek now.

Smoothing his tattered finery with a self-conscious hand, Digan reached forward to knock upon the intricate gate. His heart was pounding in his temples like the rhythm of Master Beldwyn's drums, and he could barely draw breath around the lump in his throat. His palms slick with sweat, he paused, swallowing hard and wiping them on the hem of his tunic. He closed his eyes to steel himself to continue. "Come, come," he chided himself with a growled exhortation. "What have you to lose?"

He threw back his shoulders, opened his eyes, and reached forward once more to knock upon the gate. Before his hand touched it, the mighty portal swung open upon soundless hinges. Taking a deep breath, as if about to plunge into a murky pool, Digan stepped between the panels.

Dungeons are dark. Somehow, I never really thought

about that fact before. Sitting against the cold stone wall, chin propped on her bent knees, Allysian was thinking about it a *lot* at present.

There wasn't much else to do.

She reflected upon the reason she was in this fix.

I should never have stolen that bun. I was not cut out to be a thief. I could have worked for it after all. Why did I try to do something so foolish? And the trial—if you could call it that...dragged before a magistrate and not allowed to speak up for myself. If they had only let me explain! But, no. Sentenced to four months in this hole for vagrancy...and who knows what trouble Digan will get himself into in that great span of time?

To her acute dismay, and despite her vehement objections, the guards relieved her of Digan's recorder before tossing her into the cell.

Of course, to react by kicking the magistrate in a particularly vulnerable region was probably not the wisest possible course of action. She glanced ruefully at the length of stout chain that fettered her right ankle securely to the wall. *In my own defense, I am not used to being manhandled in such a fashion, and I was terrified they would discover my secret—though how shall I keep it for so long in here? And the justification doesn't alter the fact that I am well and truly stuck here.*

Of all the deucedly stupid situations. I came all this way to save Digan, and wound up in need of rescuing myself.

To top it off, Freitanya pledged her solemn word that Allysian would find Digan here in Nausa. *But how can I hope to do that from a prison cell? Either the witch was mistaken, or she was lying.*

Allysian stoutly refused even to consider a third possibility: that her own ineptitude led to unforeseen circumstances that altered the expected outcome.

The princess sighed heavily, and shifted position, stretching out flat with her back against the wall. One good thing about the perpetual darkness; it made it easier to sleep away her troubles.

Somehow, some way, Mordigan Bryre will get me out of this mess.

She held the strictest confidence in that fact. Closing her eyes, she whispered, "Hurry, Digan, please..." and fell fast asleep.

Once Mordigan passed the inner edge of the gates, they swung closed behind him with the same silent grace. He noted this fact with an uneasy sideward glance.

Well, I'm for it now, it seems. Whether I like it or not. It is too late to turn back.

All around him the blue crystal walls blazed with the reflection of the setting sun. The crimson and gold of the sun's rays deepened much of that blue to violet and royal purple, but the highest turrets were still brilliant azure tipped with sharply pointed gilt roofs. He spun in a circle, reveling in the beauty of it. His fingers twitched for the feel of lute strings.

It is truly an awesome sight.

The sheer splendor of the keep called to the poet in his soul, and he longed for an instrument to play with an almost physical hunger. *Even the recorder would do...*

"You there!" The gruff shout froze Digan in his tracks. He whirled to face the direction of the hail.

Frantically searching for the speaker, his attention was drawn at last to a figure leaning down from an upper window. "What do you want?" the figure continued.

Squinting against the glare of the sun on the crystal, Digan raised his hand to shade his eyes. It was difficult to see the man clearly. "I-I seek Talthos," Digan stammered.

"Speak up, boy! I can't hear you when you mumble." The man sighed. "I suppose you'd better come inside. It's undignified to shout at each other like fishmongers." The figure disappeared, and Digan shifted uneasily.

Can this be the wizard? Is this the mighty Talthos? He certainly seems forbidding enough.

He raked a hand through his hair and tried to straighten his tunic. *What kind of impression will I create to so mighty a mage? Would Talthos even bother to listen?*

Before he could speculate further, the door at the foot of the crystal tower flew open, and the old man stood framed in the entryway, arms folded across his chest and a glowering frown creasing his brow.

Digan gulped and bowed low, studying the man through the fringe of his lashes. The old man was dressed in a flowing robe of a pale blue that dimly echoed the splendor of the crystal despite its over-washed pallor. His hair was iron gray around the crown of his head, but the top of his pate was bare as an egg. Bushy eyebrows met in a scowl as he continued to glare down his sharp nose at the boy.

"You may step inside and state your business, boy—but we don't need any laborers, and I don't believe in charity."

Mordigan's face grew hot. He took a deep breath and drew himself up proudly. "I came, as I was told to do, to seek Talthos. I did not come for charity, though I do not disdain work. I see, however, that it would waste both our time to continue." He turned to leave the courtyard, furious with himself for being so stupid as to hope there might be a chance of success in his mission.

A quiet voice spoke from the shadows of the interior. "Wait, boy. I will deem for myself what wastes my time."

A second figure stepped forward out of the darkness, laying an affectionate hand on the old man's shoulder in passing. "It is all right, Bariman, my friend. I will speak with the boy."

Digan gulped and snatched off his cap. He endeavored to stand straighter, very conscious of his worn velvet and rumpled silk as the immaculate wizard studied him gravely; his gray eyes cool and shadowed. Digan returned Talthos' stare in turn, regarding the magic-user squarely. The wizard looked down at him, an odd sensation for the tall boy.

Talthos' hair was a true burnished silver rather than mere gray, but there were few other signs of age in the thin, scholarly face, although Digan knew he was once court wizard to Vasileios' father. His shoulders stooped a little, as if rounded by study, but his elegant hands wore the hard look of use about them.

"What is your name, boy?" asked the servant Bariman in an officious tone, leafing through the pages of a large notebook he pulled from somewhere beneath his voluminous robes. He stood, quill poised above a page, one foot tapping an impatient cadence.

"My name is Mordigan Bryre—"

Talthos' eyes darkened, and he fell back a step before recovering himself. "Why have you come here, boy?" he murmured in a hoarse whisper, the words barely audible.

"I was told you—never mind," Digan sighed, turning to leave. "It was foolish to come. I don't know what I thought."

The wizard reached out as if to touch him, and then drew back his hand. "What were you told, Mordigan Bryre? And by whom?"

"I was told that the lute you made for my master—for Cormeyer Stareyes—as a royal bequest was magical, and that you might be persuaded to craft me such an instrument of my own. As to who sent me, I-I cannot say. I gave my word."

The wizard's eyes narrowed. "I can guess who would send you here, to me. I sense Freitanya's hand behind this game."

Digan feigned nonchalance. "I've never met the lady—" he began, but his throat shut upon the lie, and he could not continue.

"Indeed." The wizard turned, beckoning Digan to follow. "I will consider your request, Mordigan Bryre, but a question comes to mind. What will you give me for this lute you seek?"

Digan's heart fell into his boots. *What was I thinking? Of course he will require payment. And I hoped...what?*

"I have nothing to give you, lord," Digan murmured,

fingering his flat purse with regret. *How desperately foolish I was to come here!* "I should not have come."

"Have you nothing of value to offer me?"

Digan shook his head with a weary sigh, contemplating the climb back down the cliff. "Nothing."

"Then I cannot help you," Talthos stated, with a dismissive wave of his hand.

"I'll work for it!" Digan implored, hating the pleading tone in his voice, and yet unable to give up so easily when he worked so hard to get here. "I'm not afraid of hard work. Please—"

Talthos looked down his nose at the young bard. "It seems to me you do not desire the outcome badly enough to merit the waste of my magic. The spell is a difficult one, and depletes a great deal of energy. You offer me an errand boy in return. I have no need of your services. Go back from whence you came, Mordigan Bryre."

"I can't," admitted Digan with a rueful grimace. "There is nowhere left for me to go. If you do not wish to grant my petition, that is your right. Forgive me for wasting your time." He bowed to the wizard, and then started for the door, bitterly disappointed, but determined not to beg.

"A moment, boy—" Talthos called after him. "Perhaps I am too hasty. Sometimes the talent involved is worthy of such a gift on its own merit. Show me why I should reconsider my refusal. Sing me a song."

Mordigan was disconcerted by the request. Although he was used to singing with Master

Cormeyer's accompaniment, it was usually only after practicing for at least an hour before time. *Sometimes I sing for myself without preparation, but to do so for such an honored personage as Talthos?*

"What is the matter with you, boy?" snorted Bariman, an edge of impatience burring his voice. "The master wishes to hear you sing!"

Taking a deep breath and closing his eyes, Digan pretended he was singing before the court. The first piece he performed was a rollicking melody that was one of Vasileios' favorites. Thoughts of the king drifted into thoughts of Allysian, and he sang next the ballad he began composing on the day this all began. *Was that really less than a week gone?* As the last sweet note faded into silence, his eyes fluttered open.

Talthos was staring at him as if he were a poisonous snake.

Digan gulped. "D-did I do something wrong, sir?" he asked, his voice breaking with an anxious squeak.

The wizard gave himself a visible shake. "No. No, boy. You have done nothing wrong. You sing beautifully. The talent is raw, the gift not fully developed, but it is worthy of cultivation. I will make you your lute, Mordigan Bryre."

Digan's face lit up with a rare, open smile far removed from the arrogant smirk by which most people knew him. "Oh, thank you, sir!"

"It will not be a gift. You will have to earn it."

"What must I do?" asked Digan, his voice vibrating with eagerness.

"First, you must acquire certain items required for the construction—I do not propose to go gallivanting about the countryside collecting bits of wood and stone. The acquisition will be difficult, perhaps dangerous. Not all who venture thus return. Secondly, you will keep the origin of the instrument a secret. I do not desire to be inundated with petitioners. Will you agree to meet these conditions?"

"If it lies within my power, my lord," Digan answered. A respectful impulse sent him to one knee before the magic-user with his head bowed. "I am yours to command. Just tell me what I must do."

Dungeons are also dank.

Allysian sneezed violently, drawing her sleeve across her face for lack of a handkerchief.

What I wouldn't do to be snug at home in my own rooms at the palace; warm, content...and well fed. That is the worst part of this whole adventure. Even the limitations of this chain aren't as bad as the constant gnawing of my stomach.

And she knew her hunger was nothing compared to that which many of the poor suffered daily. Although the meals served here were rather skimpy, they were nourishing and palatable. She knew many of her own subjects were not so fortunate in their diet.

If I ever do get back to the safe confines of my own kingdom, I will see if I can do something about that...somehow.

She heaved a loud sigh.

If only there was something for me to do here and now! The unrelieved boredom is driving me mad.

She couldn't explore more than three feet in any direction because of the chain, and it was too dark to see anything besides. The only break in the daily monotony was when they brought the meals.

Allysian stretched out on her back, hands linked behind her head, and stared up into the darkness. The only distraction left to her was retreat into her thoughts, and she sought that solace now. As usual—particularly under the present circumstances—her thoughts turned to Mordigan Bryre.

She indulged herself in a fond remembrance of an incident many years before, quite probably the first day that she determined she was hopelessly in love with the apprentice. She was infatuated with him before that afternoon, but it didn't crystallize into something deeper until he took the blame for something she did in order to spare her the punishment...

They were playing in the king's study. It was forbidden, but she coaxed him into joining her while Cormeyer was closeted with Vasileios. Digan was nine, and she was seven. The boy was just beginning to feel that he was too old to fool with little girls, and it took a royal commandment to get him to agree.

They were engaged in a rousing game of tag when Allysian accidentally knocked over the inkwell on the desk. Exclaiming in dismay, she tried to mop up the rapidly spreading pool of ink, but only succeeded in ruining several state documents that lay upon the desktop. Sinking to the floor in a flood of wretched tears, her sleeves black with ink, she was inconsolable, but Digan tried. Oh, how he tried...

And then he rose from his squat at her side and dipped his own hands and cuffs in the ink with great deliberation, liberally splashing it onto his clothes and tucking one of the ruined sheets of parchment into the back of his belt. He was still standing at the desk when the door to the study opened, and Vasileios entered with Master Cormeyer.

With a wink at Allysian, concealed by the desk, Digan went into an act worthy of the king's own players. He jumped back from the table with a guilty start, and hid his hands behind his back.

When the king saw the chaos on the desktop, he called the boy to him. Head hanging, a sullen scowl marring his features, Digan went to the men.

"What do you have behind your back, my boy?" Vasileios questioned in stern accusation.

"Nothing," Digan muttered, but a quick examination disclosed the ruined document, and the ink-stained hands. Master Cormeyer seized the boy by the arm, and shook him roughly.

The king's anger was more controlled, but no less severe. "Take the boy home, Cormeyer. He is not to return to the palace unless he is performing. There will be no more unsupervised visits."

Cormeyer bowed, his hand tightening on Digan's upper arm until the boy grunted in pain. "As you command, sire."

Allysian, peeking over the edge of the desk as Digan was led away in disgrace was favored with another wink from the boy. Her heart flew out of her chest and rested in his hand. He was a much better thief than she.

Vasileios followed the others out, giving the princess a chance to slip away and clean herself up before she was caught.

Several days later, she saw Digan performing at a

concert, and was dismayed to see the fading ochre of a bruise under one eye and a betraying stiffness to his usually graceful movement. When she managed to maneuver a chance to speak to him, he stifled a cry as her hand touched his shoulder, but shrugged off her concern as unnecessary.

She found out later from one of the other boys that he was given ten lashes for the offense, and went without supper for a week.

She never forgot that afternoon's sacrifice. Here in the darkness of the dungeon, she could feel her face grow hot as she remembered the conclusion of the affair—an ardent kiss dropped onto Digan's cheek and the startled look in his emerald eyes as he stepped back in dismay.

I saw the realization hit him. As surely as if Papa had issued a proclamation. You must not presume...

After that, the gulf opening between them broadened into something unbridgeable. So, she took up the lute to be near him, at least for those few precious moments a week that comprised her lessons.

Allysian knew the deepest secret that Mordigan hid beneath his arrogance. His true heart was fine and noble, and he felt a desperate yearning to belong to someone. Cormeyer treated the boy more as a pet than a prodigy to his face—despite the pain she witnessed after Digan's banishment—and she saw the devastation in Digan's eyes when the master proclaimed his talent to be a negligible thing. Digan owned only his pride and his music, and Cormeyer belittled them both.

If only Digan *could have seen Cormeyer's pain as he surveyed the empty loft. Why was it so difficult to tell each other the truth? For all of us?*

How she wished that she were out of this deuced dungeon, so that she could get back to the business of finding her errant knight and bringing him home where he belonged—to her.

CHAPTER 4

DIGAN PRESSED UP AGAINST an enormous rock looming outside a yawning black cavern. He shivered beneath his thin cape, but it was more than the chill end-of-summer dawn that made him tremble. The weeks of travel since he left the enchanted walls of Azure City blurred like lightning in his memory, shimmering into each other in a headlong, breathless adventure that he did not care to remember in detail. However, the large sack tossed to the ground behind him already held most of the necessary components that would form the instrument, and he was grateful that things were going well so far.

But now he faced his greatest test yet. The rising sun gilded the rock he crouched behind, and made the shadows surrounding the mouth of the cave seem even more ominous in their brooding darkness.

Chewing his lip, as was his habit when thinking, Digan threw the long hair out of his eyes with an absent gesture. If collecting the ebony and the seven small fragments of rosewood, which would inlay the lute, were difficult ventures, the task before him seemed impossible.

The cavern outside which he crouched was the lair of a fully-grown chimera. Like its cousin the griffin, the chimera was a hybrid beast, with the head of a lion and the torso of a goat. A serpent replaced its tail, and it was rumored that the snake could spit venom at an enemy. All in all, not a beast for inspiring courage, and Digan was expected to return to Talthos with several of its teeth.

It was not an appealing proposition. Digan didn't expect it very likely that the creature would volunteer to donate the required articles, and he could think of no earthly plan to go about harvesting the fangs of an unwilling beast.

There was a soft whisper of motion from the dark maw before him, and then a resonant bass voice drawled, "Well, don't just stand there, boy. I haven't got all day to waste, you know."

Digan started, tripped over the sack of wood, and wound up seated on the ground, scrambling backwards on his hands. A low-throated chuckle reverberated from the cave mouth, and a flicker of movement translated itself into the majestic figure of the chimera. It stepped forward with delicate clicks of its great cloven hooves against the stones scattered before the cave. A pair of wings was furled against its withers. The fur of its muzzle was grizzled and there were streaks of gray in its tangled mane. Its serpent tail lashed back and forth like an independent creature, a speculative gleam in its tiny gimlet eyes. Snake-like, its tongue flicked the air toward Digan as its breath hissed past sharp fangs.

The chimera shook its head, grinning at him with far too many teeth. It took one look at Digan's face, and the throaty chuckle burgeoned into a full-blown roar of laughter. "Oh...forgive me," the creature apologized with a breathless gasp, wiping tears from its eyes with the tip of one wing. "That was abysmally rude of me, but you look so silly scuttling backward like a crab. Whatever is the matter with you, lad? You look as though you expect me to eat you."

Digan's mouth hung open in astonishment. Whatever he expected to find, this was not it.

The chimera cocked its head to one side with a quizzical frown. "Well, boy? Why have you disturbed me so early in the morning?"

Digan took a deep breath, and rose to his feet, brushing at his clothes with an automatic hand. "G-good day, sir," he began, sketching a hesitant bow. "I was sent by Lord Talthos—"

"Is that old reprobate up to his tricks again?" the chimera interrupted. "Gracious, boy, what did you—" The beast stepped closer, peering at Digan with a near-sighted squint. "What is your name, lad?"

"M-my name is Mordigan Bryre."

"Ahh...that explains it." The creature gave a sage nod of its head. "And what has Talthos sent you here to do, Mordigan Bryre?"

Digan hung his head, a dull flush suffusing his tan cheeks. "To collect..." He took another deep breath; then hurried on. "To collect teeth, sir."

"I see..." the chimera purred, its eyes glowing cat-like as the serpent coiled between its wings. "No wonder you look like you are on your way to the dining table. Don't worry, child. I'm too old for such foolishness. It was different once," it sighed.

Suddenly, its wings snapped open, and it sprang up onto its back haunches with a roar. "Once I would have bitten you in two merely for the temerity of darkening my doorstep," it thundered.

Digan gulped, fighting to hide his trembling.

The beast coughed, the sound a rough growl. "But those days are long gone. Luckily for you, Talthos no longer gives the attention to the world he once did, else he would have sent you to one of my younger kin, and a succulent morsel like you would have been gobbled up quick as lightning."

Digan was beginning to have a nasty suspicion regarding Talthos' motivations for sending him on this quest. *But, on the other hand, I can't understand why the wizard would want to harm me. Was the request for the lute really enough to merit such an extreme reaction?*

"How many do you need, boy?"

"What?" The chimera's question startled him back to the present.

"How many teeth do you need?"

Digan studied the creature's fangs with a surreptitious eye. Even the smallest were at least an inch long, and as big around as his little finger, tapering to wicked points. The teeth were intended to form the pegs for the lute's strings, but Digan didn't know exactly how Talthos meant to fashion them. "Eight?" he ventured, voice tentative.

"Come with me." The chimera turned, and led the way into the shadowy interior of the cave.

The thought of entering the beast's lair was not a comforting one. *Suppose it changes its mind, and decides to eat me after all? Or sends for one of those "younger kin" to do it?*

Ah well, the boy decided, *what do I have to lose? It is rude to keep the creature waiting.*

He stepped into the cave.

The darkness seemed absolute after the sunlight, and he blinked to help his eyes adjust to the gloom. The chimera stood in a recessed alcove near the back wall of the chamber. It struck the stone at its feet with a cloven hoof. "Here, boy. Take whatever you need."

Digan moved forward and knelt before the creature. On the floor of the alcove was the skeleton of a second beast. Time long ago reduced the body to bone alone—even the fur fallen to dust. The naked jaws held a double row of sharp, pointed fangs.

"I am still using my own teeth at present, but I believe these can be spared," commented the chimera wryly. Its voice softened into a gruff rumble. "She was my mate—but it is many years now since she died."

Digan shook his head. "I couldn't disturb—"

"She's dead, boy, and her soul long fled from this dreary place. Take as many as you need. She would be honored to help you."

"But—"

"Take them now, lad...before I change my mind and decide I am hungry after all." It bared its own fangs in one of its discomforting smiles, and Digan gently pried a handful of teeth from the skull.

"Now, go away," ordered the chimera. "I am weary..."

Digan's eye strayed instinctively to the mouth of the cave, where the sunrise was warming the dusty floor of the entranceway, but he could understand the creature's need to be left alone. *If I lost Allysian, any reminder would wound me to the soul...*

"Thank you," he murmured with grave courtesy, giving *the creature a deep bow, and stepping out into the sunlight.*

Kneeling beside his sack, Digan wrapped the loose teeth in a bit of silk ripped from the hem of his ragged shirt, careful to secure them well. He shook his head ruefully at yet another blow to his sartorial elegance. The vanity that prompted him to dress in his best for Allysian's lesson was wounded to the core at what befell to his elegant finery since. The velvet doublet was ripped in countless places, and he'd lost most of one sleeve out of his silken shirt. The worst of it was the ripening sense that he could well use the services of both a laundress and a long bath.

Slipping the little packet of teeth into his belt pouch, he was reminded suddenly of Allysian's missing comb.

How can I retrieve it and get it back to her?

He felt responsible for its loss, and a black hatred for Payter boiled within Digan's breast.

There was been no call to take the trinket from my pouch, Digan thought...*though I suppose Payter never suspected its origin, or to whom it actually belonged. He probably thought I stole it myself, making it fair game. After all, a costly bauble like that would be easy to dispose of in the marketplace, and the proceeds could feed Payter's family for a month at least.*

Digan sat back with a sigh, leaning against a rock. Thoughts of the woven golden strands decorating the treasure reminded him of the princess' bright hair, the memory painful in its intensity.

That is foolish of me; he chided himself, rising to his feet. *It is not my place to daydream about Allysian.*

I will probably never see her again, for one thing. Even if I do, she is the princess, and I am merely an apprentice— and a place-less one at that. I have no right to think of her at all; though it seems she is never far from my mind of late.

Digan gathered up his bag and slung it over his shoulder with a sigh. It was two days walk back to the Azure City. His bag now contained all the items Talthos requested except one, and he expected to find it along the return road.

Talthos' instructions hinted there would be further trials once he fulfilled these duties, but all would be worth it if he could at last become the master that Cormeyer was. Digan yearned for the lute that Talthos promised, longing to play the music clamoring in his breast.

He began to walk, humming to himself as he strode along. Before he traveled half a league, he was singing his ballad to the trees, pouring his dreams into the song.

Allysian was bored stiff. *Of course, it isn't as if there is all that much to do in the confines of a dungeon. Particularly when one is chained to the wall.*

She tried striking up conversations with the other prisoners, but they were a dull, dispirited lot for the most part. It made her heart ache to see their hopelessness. She knew that many of the people locked within the cell belonged here, but there was Caitryn, for instance, whose only crime was the loss of her young husband to a forest fire. Or Orly— reminding her with bitter poignancy of Mordigan— who turned to thievery because he could earn no other livelihood. *I fear that Digan will end up the same way if I don't do something to stop it...but what can I do locked in this hole?*

She came to Nausa because Freitanya counseled her to do so, but so far there was no sign of the youth, and it was weeks since her arrest.

Papa must be beside himself with worry. It was stupid to follow Digan. What did I hope to accomplish?

Allysian groaned and let her head fall back against the stone wall. Her mind kept going around and around the same path; always returning to the question of what earthly good she could do Digan— even if she *were* free.

But I do so want to help; to pay him back for all the times he made me laugh when I was sad, encouraged me when I was frustrated, infuriated me when I needed distraction. He is a part of my life that I don't want to let go.

She never realized just how intertwined their lives were until she found herself with so much time on her hands, and nothing to do but think. *I wonder if he realizes it. I wonder if I will ever see him again. I wonder what he is doing right now...*

At that precise moment, Digan was backed up against a large tree eyeing the irate creature before him with uneasy trepidation. It was pawing the ground before it with one hoof, head lowered so that the wicked-looking tip of the horn in the center of its forehead was pointed somewhere about his midsection. Its long golden mane hung before its violet eyes, obscuring their expression, but Digan got the distinct impression that the unicorn was not pleased to see him.

It was a beautiful being, with its glittering snow-white coat and gilt mane and tail. Its hooves shone silver in the sunlight, and looked as razor sharp as the spiraled horn. Digan gulped. He was supposed to obtain strands of the unicorn's tail to weave the strings for the lute. The thick gold fibers were more like wire than hair, and he was told that they held the strength and resiliency of metal.

Talthos counseled him to creep up on the creature while it slept and pluck what he needed. Digan wondered again what Talthos' true motives might be. The instant that he neared the unicorn it leapt to its feet and turned on him, threatening him with its mighty horn.

"I-I do not wish to harm you," Digan faltered, raising empty hands to support his declaration. "I only wanted—"

"—To pull out my lovely tail by the roots it seems!" broke in the unicorn with an angry whinny. "How dare you?"

"I was sent—"

"—By whom?" interrupted the beast again, as if determined not to let the boy finish a sentence.

"By Lord Talthos, lady," Digan replied, for despite its ferocity, he could see that the unicorn was a mare.

She gave a dismissive snort. "Talthos again? He should have strands enough to weave a rug by now! Why are you really here, boy?"

"I speak true, lady," protested the boy, stung—as always—to be disbelieved when he was being honest. "The wizard will make for me a lute—"

"And you desire my tail for strings. Has the man no original thoughts? He is always sending callow youths on this fool's errand in hopes that I will spare him the trouble of dispatching them himself, and yet he constantly forgets that my very nature precludes such behavior on my part. I cannot mortally wound an innocent. I thought the last time he—here, wait a minute, boy... You haven't been this way before, have you?"

"No, lady."

"You look familiar. What is your name, boy?"

Digan suppressed the sigh of aggravation that rose to his lips.

Perhaps it is more of my vanity that has always made me feel my looks were rather unusual...but everyone I meet on this quest seems to find them overly familiar. As if mistaking me for someone else...

"My name is Mordigan Bryre—"

"Ah, that explains it."

"Explains *what?*" he cried in frustration. The statement was beginning to be the inevitable follow-up to his introduction, and that was beginning to grate on his nerves as well.

"You mean you don't know, boy?" asked the unicorn, in a far gentler tone than she used before. "Ah well, it is not my place to say. Ask Talthos why he *really* sent you here. Come with me."

She led him to a bramble bush covered with fine wisps of hair and strands of golden mane and tail. "My curry comb," she commented in a dry tone. "I suppose briars are good for something." The speculative look she gave him imbued the words with double meaning. "Take what you need."

Digan stepped forward toward the bush, and the

unicorn called sharply, "Boy!"

Startled by her outcry, Mordigan turned, and she plunged the needle-sharp tip of her horn into his breast, sinking it to a depth of an inch. The pain was agonizing, and he sank to his knees, impaled upon the horn.

Digan stared down at the bloodstain spreading across his silken shirtfront in dull surprise. *Will it end here? She said that she could not kill an innocent... does that mean I have fallen further than I feared?*

The excruciating pain flared with each beat of his heart.

"It is as I thought," the unicorn murmured in a voice filled with silver bells. "I sense no evil in your heart, though there is much foolish wickedness. Do you love, boy?" Her eyes glowed with violet fire.

Digan fought to breathe against the pain. The violet glow was mesmerizing, but some part of him still sought to deny the truth he dared not acknowledge. "No, lady," he gasped, one sluggish hand rising to his constricting throat.

Suddenly, the pain was gone—from his chest, from his throat, even the last lingering remains of the beating at Payter's hands. The unicorn stepped back. He would have sworn she was smiling.

"Your father's son," she nodded, and Digan's heart leapt up.

"Did you know my father?" he asked with breathless urgency, leaning forward.

"What must be done will be—what will be done must be," she replied with a cryptic chuckle. "When you should know, you shall discover. You have a fine soul, Mordigan Bryre. Sleep now..." She touched the tip of the bloodied horn to his forehead, and Digan felt his eyes slide inexorably shut.

He slumped sideways to rest upon the soft grass of the glade, and his last conscious impression was of a soft sweet whisper: "You love well, Mordigan Bryre."

He dreamt of a field of sunlit heather. The sky was a blue of piercing intensity. The air was so clear and sweet it seemed almost palpable. At the edge of the field, back resting against a tree, sat a young man playing upon a lute.

Digan thought at first that he dreamt of himself—for the slim figure wore his hair and eyes—but as the dream progressed, he saw that the other was slightly older than he, broader in shoulder, and with a crooked grin quite unlike his own. The musician played the lute like a master, the sound lyrical in the crystal air. And he played Digan's song—the song not yet sung for anyone but Freitanya and the wizard.

In a clear voice of baritone, not tenor, timbre, the unknown sang the words to the two verses...and from the casual assurance with which the musician played, it was undeniably his tune.

Digan moaned without waking—even this he had lost. The song was not his own.

As the unknown sang, a beautiful young woman—with hair so pale as to appear white, despite her youth—came strolling toward him through the blooming heather. She balanced a small, dark-haired boy-child upon her hip. Her face was luminous with her love for the lutanist, and when she sank down beside him in the heather, the musician set aside his lute and took the babe from her. She nestled against his side as he bounced the little boy upon one knee, and the lutanist kissed the top of her fair head.

They were the very picture of a loving family... and, in his sleep, Digan wept.

He awoke refreshed, feeling better than he had for days, perhaps weeks. All of his aches and pains were gone, and the last of his bruises faded. There was still a jagged, bloodstained tear in the breast of his shirt to prove that the encounter with the unicorn was not also a dream, but the wound her horn made was now merely a small, darkened scar above his heart, shaped rather like a flower. He touched the spot, fingertips trembling with wonder.

I did not think I would survive the pain when first she struck me...

Pulling himself together, Digan set about harvesting the bits of unicorn mane clinging to the thorn bush. He gathered all the shining stands he could see. The fibers were stiff and coarse in texture, but surprisingly flexible and supple. He amused himself with braiding various thicknesses of cord as he continued on his journey back to the Azure City. He could approximate by feel the correct gauges for his lute strings, and it would save time to have them woven when they were called for.

As he strode along, Digan's thoughts kept drifting back to his dream. The figures stirred long forgotten memories, and he was sure in his heart that he knew that place and those people sometime long ago.

The lutanist played with a skill that aroused his deepest envy. The rippling notes continued to play in his head. *Can I dare to hope I might one day claim such a talent? Was the man my father? Was the woman my mother?*

He yearned to believe so. She was so beautiful... and the tender love on her face as she smiled down at the child had taken his breath away.

How I wish I could remember them. I remember so little of what happened before Cormeyer took me in as apprentice. If only I owned some small trace of them—something I could hold in my heart. Perhaps I wouldn't feel so alone...

Digan's fingers continued to braid the unicorn hair as he walked, their subconscious movements swift and sure. His hands were beautiful things, fine-boned and strong, eloquent in motion. The long fingers owned a delicacy of touch belied by his tendency to strike out when thwarted. With a musical instrument between those fingers, the results were magical—even without Talthos' enchantment, and despite Cormeyer's dismissive ridicule. Digan could play any instrument he set his mind to, but since childhood he preferred the lute to the lyre. *I wonder if perhaps that might result from some long-forgotten childhood memory...*

Between his preoccupation with his thoughts, and a glance down at his braiding, he did not see the girl until he very nearly stumbled into her cook fire.

"Take care!" she cried, shielding her stewpot. "There is little enough as it is, without a great lout like you kicking over the kettle."

"I'm sorry, I didn't see you there—"

"Obviously." The girl gave a derisive sniff. "Too fine and noble to watch where you are going, I suppose."

The rebuke was undeserved, and once the boy would have lashed back with a waspish reply, but now he curbed the response that sprang to his lips. "I am truly sorry," he apologized again. "I will not disturb your camp further." He turned to walk on, and the girl rose to her feet.

"Wait, boy—I am sorry too. I am unused to company, and forget how to behave. It is late, and no shelter you could reach by nightfall is any better than my campfire. Would you join me for the night? We can stretch the soup with tall tales and a little company." The girl smiled an invitation, cocking her head to one side with a little bird-like gesture that struck him as oddly familiar.

She was a pretty girl, tall and tan, with startling gray eyes rimmed with black, like those of a wolf. Her hair was as dark as his, but the setting sun struck copper highlights from the crown of her head.

Until that precise moment, he did not realize just how late it was. *The unicorn made me sleep longer than I thought.*

Digan smiled back at her. "The fire, and the company, would be welcome."

"Come and sit then," she grabbed his hand and pulled him to the fireside, sinking down on the leaf-strewn ground. Summer was nearly gone now...the quest for the components of his lute had consumed the latter half of the season.

He sank down beside her, and she curled up like a contented kitten, watching him with those haunting eyes. The movement bared her leg to the thigh as her slit skirt parted with distracting effect.

In fact, that dress is altogether too distracting, Digan thought, shifting uncomfortably.

It fit her snugly, baring sun-browned arms and throat, and freeing her long legs. It appeared as if sewn of dried leaves and spider silk, though he knew that could not be.

"What brings a city boy like you to my forest?" she asked, voice colored with curiosity as she leaned provocatively close. "Have you no sweetheart waiting up for you?"

Allysian's sunlit hair and grave blue eyes flashed before his memory. *But she is not mine!* He reminded himself forcibly. *She never can be. She is a princess.*

"No," he replied. There was enough untruth in the denial to send a sharp pain shooting through his throat, and he caught his breath in a hiss.

"Perhaps I should keep you here, then," she teased, with a bubbling chuckle, "to amuse me and sing me songs."

"But I cannot sing, lady," he hedged, and—for the moment—it was true, as his throat spasmed in a convulsive fit of coughing.

"You poor boy," she purred, laying a nut-brown hand against his chest in sympathy. "I know just what will fix that nasty cough of yours."

Digan flinched back, and felt the heat rising to his cheeks. "I-it is nothing, lady," he croaked hoarsely.

"Oh...I am no lady..." She moved even closer, lips parted—then sat back on her bare heels with a peal of silvery laughter. "Oh, my! The look on your face is absolutely priceless, boy! She must be some girl, this sweetheart that you haven't got."

"She is," Digan replied before he thought, and then wished he could sink into the earth and be swallowed alive.

The girl shook her head with an indulgent chuckle. "I merely meant that my soup will soothe your throat, boy. I am not so unbecoming that I must seduce unwary travelers." She moved to the cooking pot.

"Oh, no—" Digan hastened to reassure her. "You are very beautiful..."

"But your heart has been claimed by another," replied the girl, handing him a bowl of soup. "It is just as well, Mordigan Bryre."

He jerked away from her, and the hot soup scalded his hand. His heart pounded with such violence in his breast that he didn't even notice.

I know no one in this kingdom. Even if I could dismiss the fact that the chimera and the unicorn recognized my name as some miracle of their magic, I cannot explain away how she *knows it without it being given.*

There was something unnatural about this meeting, and the thought chilled his very soul.

Her eerie gray eyes drilled into him. "Yes, boy," she breathed, "I know your name. And I know what you are doing in my woods." Her face was solemn now. All the teasing familiarity was gone, leaving her regal and terrifying. "You must beware, Mordigan Bryre. Talthos will try and cheat you of your prize. It is not your fault. It is not his fault. That fault lies with one from long ago...but he will try, because he must.

"Stand up to him, and he will give in. Do not let him intimidate you. You have a right to his favor. None more so. Take him the items that you have collected, and give him this as well—" She handed him a brilliant flawless emerald set in a golden filigree formed in the shape of an ellipse. The stone was carved with an intricate design of vines and flowers. "He will know from whence it came. Tell him it is for the bridge of the instrument."

"I cannot take this, lady," Digan protested, holding the emerald out to her. "It is far too valuable."

"It is already yours, my boy," she demurred. "Now, eat what you have left of your soup before it gets cold," she ordered briskly, in a business-like manner that presented odd contrast to her appearance. "Rest well tonight, for tomorrow you must beard the lion in his den!"

Digan slipped the emerald into his pouch and did as he was told. The soup was delicious, and again there was a strange feeling of familiarity about it. His eyelids grew heavy as he ate, and by the time the bowl was empty, he was having trouble stifling his yawns. *It seems strange that I should be so tired after the nap in the unicorn's glade...*

Even as the thought struck him, his head bowed forward, and he jerked awake with an effort. The girl smiled, her face gentle, and took the bowl from his lax hand. "Sleep, Digan. Tomorrow comes apace."

He nodded, with a weary yawn, and stretched out beside the fire. His eyelids drooped as he stared into the heart of the crackling flames. *Where is Allysian tonight?* he wondered drowsily. *Does she think of me as often as I do of her? And if so, what matter of thoughts are they?*

Digan was asleep before he could speculate further on the answer.

Allysian lay full-length upon the hard stone floor of her cell, her face buried in the crook of her arm. *I tried. I tried so hard...but I can't do it anymore. I can't be strong and noble forever.*

She was still a very young princess to be on her own...especially as a chained prisoner in a foreign dungeon.

The princess commanded herself not to cry, but somehow, this time, it didn't work. Tears fell like steady rainfall onto the worn sleeve of her borrowed tunic, soaking the thin cotton. She was so alone here, and she no longer held any real hope of rescue.

I am going to rot here in this cell, and no one will ever even know the difference. It is almost a month since my capture, and the days flow on endlessly without any sign of Digan.

Papa must be thinking heaven knows what of me, and Mordigan Bryre is going on about his business with blithe indifference, as he always does. He will never even know...

Damn the man! In the space of a heartbeat, her mood swung from wallowing self-pity to righteous indignation. *How dare Digan draw me into a situation like this?*

But honesty was *not* a trait Allysian lacked, and she could not lie to herself.

Digan can't be blamed for getting me into this mess. He never encouraged my feelings. He is a perfect gentleman to me. To Mordigan, I am just a girl—no, I am just a princess—whom he treats with friendship laced with the respect due my station. But I so yearned for him to feel more than mere friendship that I read it into his behavior.

Why did I ever listen to Freitanya in the first place?

When she didn't find Mordigan in Nausa, she should have turned around at once and gone home instead of waiting for him. She could be safe and warm at home in the palace.

There, if I get bored, I can order entertainment, or purchase some new bauble from the marketplace. I can eat three square meals a day, and push away my plate half-full if so inclined. I can sleep on goose down mattresses under a satin coverlet, and dream of Mordigan Bryre...

She smiled tearfully in the darkness of the cell, swiping at her wet cheeks. That much she could still do, despite her confinement. It was easier to escape the reality of the moment when she was sleeping. In fact, it seemed like more and more of her time was spent in dreams of Digan...

How I long to see him again! Will he ever come and rescue me? Do I even want him to come to me if it will be here in this comfortless dungeon?

When Digan awoke at dawn, muzzy-headed from sleep, his immediate reaction was one of anger. He was tired of being put to sleep by almost everyone he met. It was an affront to his considerable dignity, and deucedly irritating as well. It made him feel like a small child who couldn't be trusted to go to bed on his own.

Well, I am not a child. In fact, he realized with a sudden start, *the long-awaited birthday came and went without notice—I am now eighteen...or at least that is what we always guessed.*

No one knew his exact age. Cormeyer used the day Digan was found in the square as his birthday, and the old woman who relinquished the boy into his apprenticeship was imprecise as to Digan's real age.

But in all ways that count, I am now eighteen, and a man grown.

He thought wistfully of the journeyman's papers that should have been his. *All I ever wanted from life was to be a bard...I never even contemplated another road. Now my own carelessness has thrown it all away.*

"I really must be growing up," he murmured to the empty glade, with a rueful shake of his head, "else I never would admit that the fault was mine... not even to myself."

With a sigh of resignation, Digan rose to his feet. It was still a long day's walk to the Azure City, but he was determined that he would be there by sunset. He longed for home.

Even the thought of descending the cliff no longer held the full terror it once did. He admitted at last to himself that he wanted to go home...to where a pair of blue eyes waited under a mass of golden hair. *It is selfish of me, I know, but I want the chance to reap those small scraps of affection Allysian is always so quick to offer. I might not rate a future at her side, but I can stand in her shadow...*

Digan slung his sack over his shoulder and set off at a brisk pace. The wolf girl had already gone when he awoke, but she left a handful of journey cakes and a skin of water for him. He was grateful for the gesture, and became even more appreciative as the day wore on.

The gift saved him the necessity of scavenging for luncheon, and Digan made better time than he anticipated. The sun was still level with the gilded turrets of Talthos' keep when he approached the Azure City.

Digan paused outside the gates, taking a deep breath and tightening his grip on his bag of precious treasures. He was not looking forward to the confrontation the wolf girl warned him to expect, but he was resolved to have his lute—whatever the cost.

"Do you really think it will work?" Allysian inquired, favoring the flimsy bit of metal in her hand with a skeptical frown. By now, her eyes were so used to the darkness that she could see fairly well in the gloom, but she still wasn't sure that she was up to this challenge.

"You're the thief, ain't you," rumbled the man mountain before her with a sulky growl. "Don't you know what to do with it?"

Allysian cuffed the man lightly in the arm. "Of course I do, silly," she answered, trying hard to guess. "This just isn't the type of lockpick I'm accustomed to, that's all. They don't all function the same, you know."

Despite his ominous manner and his hulking size, the princess knew the other prisoner was very gentle beneath his gruff exterior. He heard her crying one night and crept to her side to offer comfort. Of course, he thought her a frightened page boy caught thieving, and—as a consequence of this misconception—he brought her a thin, flexible lockpick to use on her ankle chain. She daren't ask where he got it. It was a good-hearted gesture in any case...but she wasn't sure how to make the best of it. She stuck the end of the pick into the lock of her fetter and began to jiggle it back and forth, pretending she knew how to go about the task.

"Are you sure you know what you are doing?" the giant muttered, bending down to peer at her ankle.

"I told you," she grunted back, twisting the metal hard in the keyhole, "it isn't what I'm used to." The metal bent in her hand, and she pulled it out of the chain with a sigh. "I'd better think about this for a while. I'd hate to break it off in the lock." She slipped the bit of metal into the front of her tunic and smiled up at him. "Thank you, Bour. It is a fine gift."

It was more than that. It was a lifeline when she needed it most. For the first time in weeks, Allysian began to feel a bit of hope.

Mordigan's face set in dark scowl. He stood before Talthos with his arms folded across his chest. "I did what you asked. I fulfilled all your requests. Here are the items I was sent for. What do you mean you will not make the lute?"

Talthos turned away with a negligent shrug. "You broke your word. You told of your quest."

"I told no one!" Digan cried.

"By your own admission you spoke of it not only with the chimera but also with the unicorn," the wizard sneered. "They are both intelligent creatures. Do they not count in your reckoning?"

"But—" began the boy, desperate to explain.

Talthos cut him off with a wave of his hand. "And what of this mysterious girl in the forest?"

"She knew my name and quest before we met!"

"How convenient for you. However, it changes nothing. You forfeited your right to my help."

"She said you would do this," Digan murmured, swallowing against the bitter bile that rose in the back of his throat. "She said that you would refuse to honor your promise."

"Very insightful, this forest vixen of yours."

"At least she told me the truth!"

"Pretty words coming from you, boy," the wizard scoffed. "I'm surprised you even recognized it. You've had so little experience with that commodity."

Digan felt the blood rush from his face. He stood frozen, dizzy with the pain of realizing that Talthos was right. The scar above his heart began to throb, and he forced himself to continue breathing.

The boy fumbled blindly in his belt pouch and pulled out the emerald. He laid it on the surface of the desk behind which Talthos stood. "The girl in the forest gave me this," he said, voice dull. "She said it was for the bridge of the lute. You may as well have it too."

The wizard reached down a shaking hand and picked up the carved stone. "Where did you get this, Mordigan Bryre?" The mage's voice was cold steel.

"I told you. The girl in the forest gave it to me, for the lute."

"Where did she get it, then?"

"I don't know. She said it was mine."

"She lied!" Talthos roared. "But now I know her name. I will deal with that one myself. Get out, boy."

Digan nodded, heart heavy. "Yes. There is nothing left for me here. Perhaps someday you will craft a fine instrument for someone more acceptable to your standards. You have all the pieces now."

He felt as if he struggled against chest-high water. His limbs were wooden and his head rang. But he vowed not to beg. "Goodbye, my lord Talthos," he murmured. "I see now the value of your word. Perhaps it is best that you hide here in your crystal fortress. That way the people of Marineaux can still honor your memory with the awe you once deserved." He turned and stumbled toward the door of the chamber, unsteady on his feet.

"What do you know of honor, Mordigan Bryre?" Talthos spat after him.

Digan turned, with his hand upon the door, his face set, his eyes sparkling with tears of disappointment he refused to shed. "I know it is all that I possess. Everything else has been stripped from me. But my honor and my pride are mine, and you shall steal neither."

"How dare you speak of honor? You who are known throughout the kingdom as a lying braggart who concocts grandiose fantasies at the drop of a hat rather than face the truth of his menial birth—what truck do you have with honor?"

Digan gulped. "I have never given my word and broken it." His voice was sure and steady, for it was the truth. "Whatever lies I may have told were never purposefully intended to cause hurt to another. I have suffered more for them than any..."

The boy sighed, with a weary shake of his head. "What is the use? You will not believe me anyway." He twisted the handle of the door.

"Wait," Talthos ordered, in a strangely choked voice.

Digan straightened his shoulders and pushed open the door, not looking back at the wizard. Digan never looked back.

He forced himself to keep moving, through the keep and out of the gate. Once outside the compound, he could bear it no longer, and he began to run.

Digan poured his rage and despair into his running, and sped for the distant cliff. The tears he was fighting spilled down his cheeks, and he dashed them away with angry swipes of his fist.

I am a grown man. I am too old to cry!

But it became harder and harder to see through the film of tears, and he was stumbling along blindly by the time he reached the cliff.

He threw himself down on the grass at the edge of the precipice, crushing the delicate star-like flowers beneath him as he gave in to the emotions ripping through him.

The wizard is right. I always prided myself on my honor above all else, and yet every lie I told whittled away at that honor until I was the only person who could not see it for the hollow shell that was left. What a fool I am! What an utter fool...

The raging tide of his emotions spent itself in time, leaving him drained and exhausted. Pillowing his head on his crossed arms, he contemplated the future with weary disillusionment.

All my hopes were pinned on returning home in triumph, bearing the magical lute as proof I was worthy of a second chance. Now that hope is gone as well.

It is as I told Allysian...there is nothing left for me in Marineaux. I could not bear to be so close to her and have no claim to her company. At least as Cormeyer's apprentice I was allowed to sing at the court. Now I will not even be given that shadowy comfort. No, I will not return to the capital.

He would seek his fortune in Nausa, and try to forget the golden waves of her hair, and the soft light of her smile. He would pretend he never knew the princess Allysian. *Perhaps, in time, I will convince myself of that lie...the greatest lie of all.*

With a groan, he realized he did not fulfill Freitanya's exhortation. *I didn't win the lute. The curse will still be active. Whether I wish to be or not, I will be an honest man from now on. Or mute.*

Perhaps that would be better. I will be far less likely to get myself in trouble if I can't open my mouth and stick my foot in it...

Melancholy thoughts whirling in his head, Digan closed his eyes. And this time, when he slept, it was at his own command.

CHAPTER 5

MORDIGAN STOOD STRAIGHT AND tall before the Nausaen court of law, chin tilted in proud defiance. The tattered silk shirt, velvet tunic with its multiple rents, and shabby leggings created a most disreputable picture, but Digan met the eye of the magistrate with a shadow of his trademark insolence. The two weeks of wandering that brought him to this pass pared flesh from his trim waist and angular cheekbones, but nothing from his spirit. He was the picture of unrepentant arrogance.

By Hathor, let it be enough to fool the judge. They must not know how utterly helpless I feel. Come, Digan... earn your reputation as wastrel. Be the arrogant thief they expect you to be...

He straightened his shoulders marginally, shifted his weight, and stifled a contemptuous yawn.

That's it, lad. They mustn't suspect the truth.

The terror he felt knotting his entrails must not show. He clenched his fists so tightly at his sides that his nails drew blood from his palms.

"Mordigan Bryre, you stand accused of vagrancy and theft. You were caught red-handed lifting this man's purse in the marketplace. How say you?"

Digan barked out a sharp burst of sound that could have been a laugh. He'd told his story three times now, and no one would listen...

After days of aimless wandering, he crossed into Nausa in hopes of starting life afresh.

"I could be a runner for you," he pleaded with a burly butcher. "I am quick on my feet, and I have a good memory for figures. I could deliver your wares to the customers."

"Don't need no one like that," the man replied, shaking his head. "And if I did, wouldn't be no stranger—especially not some beggar boy more like to eat me out of all me profits."

The comment stung. Digan's silver was long gone, and he knew he looked a mess, but there was nothing to be done about it unless he could find a way to earn a living. He bit back a rude reply, and sketched a bow instead. "Thank you, sir. I will try elsewhere."

He turned with a sigh, just in time to see a fat merchant at a nearby stall drop his purse upon the dusty street.

"Sir!" He darted over and picked up the heavy bag to return it.

The merchant glanced over and saw the purse in his hand.

Before Digan could give it back to him, the man seized the boy's wrist in a grip of iron. "Guard! Guard! This thief has stolen my purse!"

"But I didn't. You dropped it. I was just trying—"

He felt a hand clamp down on his shoulder and spin him around. The sudden momentum knocked him off balance, and he fought to keep his feet. A rock-hard fist in the side of his face helped counter his forward fall, and he staggered back into the arms of a second guardsman.

"I was just trying to give the gentleman back his purse," he gasped.

"Tell me another," sneered the first guard, *slamming that boulder on the end of his arm into the prisoner's unprotected midsection.*

The air went out of Digan in a whoosh, and he groaned. Here we go again.

Before he could protest further, he was dragged before the court...

Digan's mouth set in a stubborn line as resentful temper boiled within him. Fresh bruises on his face attested to the heavy-handed treatment of the guards. *I'm not going to dignify the charge with further denials. They don't care to hear the truth.*

"Well? Speak up, boy! Have you nothing to say in your defense?"

Digan shook his head, eyes lowered.

The magistrate glared at the boy's impudence. "You say that you were merely returning this man's gold. That should be easy enough to prove... Explain the circumstances of the incident."

Digan remained obdurately silent. *They would not believe the truth—I've tried and tried to tell it—and it would cost me far too dear to lie...*

"You really are an arrogant pup, aren't you?" The judge turned to a waiting guardsman. "Throw him in the common cell for the night. Perhaps an evening or two spent underground will loosen his tongue."

*Or still it...*thought Digan with a sour grimace, as the guard grabbed his arm in an implacable grip and jerked him out of the chamber. He trotted along beside the tall soldier, struggling to keep up with the long, loping strides. The affront to his dignity pained Digan almost as much as his arm—which was fast becoming numb beneath the crushing clutch of the guardsman's fingers.

Why doesn't he just grab my ear and have done? If he is going to treat me like an errant child, I might as well look the part!

After clattering down several steep stairways, marching through twisting tunnels of passageways, and unlocking at least three massive oaken doors, the guard came to an abrupt halt, and thrust his prisoner into a dark, dank hole. Stumbling forward in an attempt to keep his balance, Digan fell to his hands and knees—landing heavily on the stone floor.

The impact sent a jolt all the way to his shoulders, and he grit his teeth, rubbing the ache out of his bicep where the soldier manhandled him. He peered into the darkness, trying to distinguish shapes, and—after his eyes adjusted a bit—found that he was in a huge chamber hewn from solid rock. At first, there was silence, and then he began to hear little whispers all around him.

I am not alone.

Gaze darting from side to side as he tried to look ten directions at once, he spotted the glint of eyes in the faint light seeping through the barred aperture within the door.

I am most definitely *not alone.*

There were at least twenty people in the cell with him. Most huddled in groups of two or three, but here and there a lone figure showed as a darker shadow against the gloom.

He was a stranger in this town, and now he found himself surrounded by the worst segment of the citizenry—those who somehow earned the censure of their peers...the dregs of society...the...

"Mordigan! Mordigan Bryre! Are you really here at last?"

The urgent voice whispering his name seemed like something out of a dream—or nightmare.

Who could know me here? he wondered uneasily.

"Digan!" There was a note of exasperation in the voice now...and the use of his nickname argued that the voice knew more about him than there was a right for it to know. "Get over here!"

It was hard to ignore the imperious tone of the command. In some strange way, the very nature of it added a touch of familiarity to the summons. He crawled toward the speaker.

"Ouch! You clod! You just knelt on my hand!" The voice was thick with pain and unshed tears...and decidedly female.

Mordigan leaned forward until he was a scant inch from her face, but he still couldn't see who it might be in the dim light of the cell. "Do I know you, lady?"

"I should hope so, idiot. If not, I was even stupider than I tell myself to come after you..."

The boy frowned. *Come after me? No one knew where I went. Cormeyer didn't even give me time to send a message to the square, and Payter didn't bother to ask. I came away that day with only the clothes on my back and a handful of coins. There was only one other...*

"By the goddess...Your Highness?" he whispered in disbelief.

His heart contracted to think that it might be so. *Much as I long to see Allysian again, I would not choose these circumstances in which to do it...*

"Shh!" ordered the princess. "It's bad enough as it is. If they knew I was a girl—and royal besides—I shudder to think what they would make of that situation."

"How...why...what are you doing here?"

"I told you. I followed you. Only, I got lost. And I got hungry. They are extremely intolerant of petty thievery in this kingdom."

"You must go home."

"Why didn't I think of that?" she drawled, her voice dripping with sarcasm as she rattled a length of chain securing her ankle to the wall.

Mordigan's blood boiled. "How dare they?" He grabbed the chain and tried to pull it free of the masonry.

"Digan..." She laid her hand on his straining shoulder. "Digan! That won't work. I've tried."

"I...am...stronger...than you," he grunted in reply, placing one foot against the stone for leverage and tugging with all his might.

"Ohh..." she whimpered.

He dropped the chain as if it were white-hot. "Did I hurt you, my lady?" he cried, forgetting her words of caution in his anxiety.

"Shh! No, of course not. But you weren't listening to me. The chain can't be pulled from the wall. How effective would it be to have shackles the prisoners could just up and break any time they wanted to? If he couldn't pull it loose—" She pointed to a huge hulk of shadow nearby. "—Then you certainly won't be able to."

"But I must get you out of here."

"Well, that is the general hope, yes. How good are your lockpicking skills?"

"I'm a bard! Nearly..." he amended, with a slight cough. "I don't have any use for thieves' tricks."

"I was afraid of that. Well, I am a mere princess," she murmured. "We have fewer scruples. But I've tried, and I just haven't got a delicate enough touch. Here. Take this—" She took his hand and placed a slim piece of metal into it. "See what you can do with it."

With her guidance, he slipped the end of the metal sliver into the keyhole of her ankle-cuff, and maneuvered it around. He worked by touch alone, and it was deucedly difficult. Without thinking, he took her ankle into his lap, and bent over the task, focusing his will on the attack. Finally, he was rewarded by a dull click.

"You did it!"

"Did I?" He was still rather dazed by the whole affair.

"Yes. Now, open the cuff—oww! Here...let me." She bent forward and snapped open the shackle, wriggling her foot with a blissful sigh. "Ahh! Much better. Um...Digan?"

"Yes, Highness?"

"You can let go of my foot now."

"Hathor's Harp! Of course—" He released her, and beat a hasty retreat.

"Thank you. I don't think I could have stood much more of that." Using the wall to brace against, she rose shakily to her feet. "That feels so good!" She stretched muscles stiffened by confinement, and Digan watched in bemusement, noticing that his eyes were becoming much more adjusted to the gloom. He could make out the starlight glimmer of her hair—much less of it than the last time he saw her—and the fact that she offered the slim silhouette of a page boy, rather than the bulk of court dress.

"Y-you are wearing a doublet and hose—"

She laughed at him. "Well, you would hardly have expected me to come after you in a court gown, would you?"

"I never expected you to come after me at all," he answered with frank candor. "Why did you?"

Allysian turned away from him, pacing several steps. She refused to face him. "I-I was worried about you. Master Cormeyer was unfairly harsh, and Papa a fool to back him. I knew no one else would give a damn..."

She glanced over her shoulder—he could see the pale oval of her face...and thought perhaps she smiled. "You didn't go out of your way to make many people like you, did you?"

He was glad now of the darkness. It hid the blood rushing to his cheeks.

That seems to be the general opinion. And it is accurate. Among the boys, I was feared, certainly, perhaps admired, but not liked...and even the Master turned away from me in the end.

"I guess not," he admitted with a sigh, staring down at the stone floor.

Digan jerked back at the touch of a hand on his shoulder, but it was Allysian, kneeling beside him. "You never let yourself *be* yourself because you are so afraid of being hurt. But I know your heart, Mordigan Bryre. Even if you do not." He felt her hand brush against his hair, and heard a soft whisper of breath in his ear—so soft he was unsure of its reality— "And I love you for it."

Did I actually hear those words, or did my own fancy merely put my thoughts into her voice? When he would question her on the matter, there was a sudden susurration of sound throughout the cell, and she scrambled back into her position against the wall.

"Quick!" she hissed. "Get away from me. The guards are bringing food. They mustn't find out we know each other."

Ever obedient to her commands, he moved some distance away to the center of the cell where he could keep an eye on her. There was a clanging outside the door, and it flew open.

Two guardsmen entered, armed with whips, and took up menacing positions on either side of the opening. The light streaming into the cell from the guttering torches in the hallway half-blinded Digan, and he threw up an arm to shield his eyes.

All around him, he could hear scurrying movement. It appeared that more of the prisoners were free to move about as he was than chained to the walls like Allysian.

What did she do to merit such precautions? Do I really want to know?

A third figure entered the cell, his huge girth blocking out the light for a moment. He carried a cast iron cauldron as if it were a pastry dish, and began to ladle out the contents into bowls held up in eager hands. As he made his way around the cell, Digan took advantage of the greater light to sneak a peek at Allysian.

She was cowering against the wall, hiding her feet beneath her to aid the deception that she was still chained. Her long, glorious hair was hacked off about her chin, and she was wearing a shapeless doublet of dark green, with black hose.

My colors, he thought. *As a matter-of-fact, those look suspiciously like my clothes...*

She caught him looking at her, and frowned, giving her head a slight shake of warning—then winked and smiled to show she didn't really mind.

He took the point, and glanced away, to find the fat cook standing before him. "Where's yer bowl, boy?"

"I-I haven't got one."

The cook gave a grunt of laughter. "Then you don't eat. I reckon they must want to tame you a bit first. You'll come down off your high horse when you're hungry enough."

To be honest, Digan was quite hungry now...the scent of stew wafting from the pot made his mouth water. The last of the wolf girl's journey cakes was eaten two days ago, despite his careful husbandry.

But I am not about to beg for food, and if they think they can break me so easily, they are sadly mistaken.

The cook shrugged, and carried his cauldron toward the door. Digan took advantage of his exit to make one last quick survey of the cell with his eyes, concentrating on burning its contours into his brain— it was a rough circular chamber dug from living rock, and the magistrate said the cell was underground.

There are no windows, and nothing I can see that would be of any use...

Then the guards exited, slamming the door closed, and he was once more in the dark. But at least, this time, he knew he was not alone. He crawled back to Allysian's side.

"Oww!" She punched him lightly in the arm. "Are you going to make a habit of kneeling on my fingers? If so, I may not be so quick to rescue you."

"I'm sorry, Princess—"

"Shh!" she hissed. "I told you—we can't let anyone know who I am. Even these poor wretches might be willing to leak that information if it meant getting out of here, and I can't say I would blame them. Would you?"

"No, my lady."

"That's just as bad! I am supposed to be a particularly obstinate page boy, who wound up in shackles for kicking the magistrate in the—well, never mind where I kicked him. The point is, you can't go around calling me 'Highness' or 'my lady.' Call me...Sian. That could be a boy's name."

"Whatever you say, High—Sian." He felt awkward calling her by a diminutive of any kind, but he could see her point.

"Here—" She thrust her bowl at him. "I've eaten what I want. You take the rest."

"I couldn't—"

"Don't get high-and-mighty with me, Mordigan Bryre—or noble and self-sacrificing either. I'm not hungry, and there's no need to waste the food. If you don't want it, I'll give it to one of the others—"

"No...I'll take it. Thank you." The stew was

surprisingly good under the circumstances. *If this kingdom can afford to feed its prisoners this well, it must be rich indeed...*he wolfed it down.

"I knew you were hungry," she commented, and he could hear the smile he could not see in the gloom. "Now, let's get out of here." She wound the chain in a neat coil against the wall and stood up.

He rose to his feet, topping her height by several inches. "How? We are in an underground dungeon, with a locked door guarded by very large men with very sharp swords."

"Yes," she replied. "We *are* underground. Believe me, I am well aware of that fact. I've had plenty of time to digest that fact. I've been here for about a month myself."

The casual revelation made him dizzy with shock. *She was languishing in chains almost the entire time I was about my quest. Her father will be—I cannot bear to think what Vasileios will be imagining.*

Digan's mind reeled. The thought of what she must have suffered broke his heart. *How much worse must the king be feeling? And with the king's temper, I hate to imagine what kind of reception I will have when I return her to her rightful place...but return her I will.*

Digan resolved to get the girl back to Marineaux with all possible haste...by whatever means necessary.

He came to the dazed realization that Allysian was still speaking, and he forced his attention back to her words.

"I don't know what your teachers told you," the princess continued, "but my tutor told me that no living being could breathe without fresh air. There are about thirty people in this cell."

Mordigan mumbled under his breath, "I had no teachers..." He was ashamed of the admission. "All I know is my music."

Allysian placed a hand on his chest. "I'm sorry, Digan. I didn't mean to imply..."

"But it's true...Sian. I am woefully ignorant. I-I never thought it mattered much about books and writing...until Master Cormeyer threw me out. I can read and write my notes, but not the letters. I wish...I wish I'd learned more."

"I'll teach you, if you'd like," the girl offered, her voice shy.

"Do you mean that?"

"Of course! I never say anything I don't mean."

Mordigan wondered if that were true...*and if it is, did I really hear those whispered words?*

"But first, we have to get out of here." Her voice took on the no-nonsense briskness of one used to giving commands. "As I was saying, no living creature can breathe without fresh air. The room would be stuffy—well, stuffier than it is—if the doorway was the only air supply for this many people. There must be some shaft or something bringing in air...all we have to do is find it—" She was pacing the room as she spoke, peering up at the ceiling with a frown of intense concentration. Digan, following her, almost ran into her as she came to an abrupt halt. "There!" She pointed upward. "Do you see it?"

Voice filled with excitement, she whirled around, and knocked against him, he was so close behind her.

Digan steadied her as she lost her balance, and she looked up into his eyes. Even in the dark, he could see—then she cleared her throat, and stepped away from him.

"There's a shaft up there. See that slightly lighter square of space." She pointed upward. "It must twist several times, because I've never seen any daylight filtering in, but I see it...I know I do. All we have to do now is get to it."

"That is easier said than done, my—Sian. How do you propose we manage it? It must be twenty feet to the ceiling. And even then, what if it leads straight up? How will you climb out?"

"We'll worry about that detail when we get to it," she answered, her tone confident of success. "But we're going to need help."

Allysian began to circulate among the prisoners, bending down to examine each face in turn. She held murmured conversations with several of them, and they rose and shuffled to where Digan stood. Soon, there was quite a large group around him.

She came back to a position beneath the shaft, and outlined her plan with swift efficiency. "We need to build a living mountain here," she explained. "The base must be strong enough to support Mordigan's weight. Digan, when the pyramid is high enough, you must climb up to the shaft and see how it is formed. With any luck, one of the first twists is right above us, and the shaft slopes or travels sideways for a distance. Of course, if it should be straight-up vertical, you will have to climb it like a chimney—do you know how?"

"Aye. I've climbed a few of those in my time. 'Tis easy enough." The lie exacted its toll, and he winced at the fiery pain in his throat.

"Good. You will need to climb until you come to the first twist, so we will know what we are dealing with."

"It is a good plan, but you are much lighter than I am, why don't you go up first?"

"Because you can pull me up into the shaft if necessary—but I can't lift you."

The argument was a logical one. He nodded.

"Now, we must hurry—but you have to be very quiet. The guards won't come back in tonight unless they hear something unusual, but we can't afford to be caught. If this works," she told the other prisoners solemnly, "we will get help. I promise that you will be rescued."

Digan glanced at their fellow captives, heart filled with unease. *It is a pretty gesture, but there may well be a reason why some of these fellows are incarcerated... after all, it is a prison cell...*

"Let's go!" Allysian commanded, and the pyramid formed obediently before her. "Digan— up you go."

Digan closed his eyes and took a deep breath.

I leave it in your hands, Lady Hathor...

He opened his eyes and steadied himself on the shoulder of the man kneeling before him. Focusing all his attention on the task at hand, Digan planted his booted foot on the first step of the human ladder.

I've never told a soul about my fear of heights. I mustn't fail Allysian now when she needs me so. She must not find out that what she is asking is one of the hardest tasks I've ever faced.

The image of a tear-stained little face pointing up at a kitten stranded in a tree flashed through his thoughts.

I've done it for her before. I can do it again.

The wobbling structure before him did not inspire his confidence...but he climbed up, heart in mouth, conscious of the fact that she was counting on him to get them out.

The top tier of the pyramid ended four feet below the opening.

No! I can't. It is too much. Please...

"Are you all right?" came an anxious little voice from too far beneath him.

Digan steeled himself for the next task. "I'm fine. Just resting a moment."

I must go on. For her sake. I must get her home safely.

Taking a deep, shuddering breath, he planted his feet as securely as possible, and straightened up with slow caution, trying desperately not to look down.

It was precarious rising up into the mouth of the shaft, and his heart almost jumped out through his throat when he overbalanced. He grabbed for the edge of the rock and caught himself, sucking in gasping lungfuls of air until he could calm his shaking.

The lip of the shaft hit Digan in the center of the chest as he stood upright, and he leaned against the relative safety of the rock, grateful for the support. It was definitely a lip. The shaft took a sharp bend about six inches up, sloping upward out of his line of sight. If he could pull himself into the opening, it should be simple to climb up into the tunnel.

The angle was extremely awkward. He couldn't get a good purchase on the rock, and it was only by pushing off from the pyramid beneath him with a little jump that he could lift himself at all. There was a bad moment where Mordigan hung in mid-air by his straining arms, swinging like a dying pendulum.

No. I mustn't fall! I mustn't. There is no one else to get her home.

Grunting with the exertion, he coaxed one more bit of leverage out of his trembling arms, and managed to raise himself into the passageway. He lay trembling and spent, fighting to catch his breath, until he could trust himself to speak. Shakily, he rose to a sitting position, and then leaned over the lip to call to the princess.

"Come up, Sian." Digan reached toward her, and she scrambled up the pyramid. Her head just cleared the lip of the tunnel, and Digan's heart sank.

I am going to have to haul her up bodily...and if I am not careful, her weight will drag me to my own death—or at least cause me serious injury—when I hit that stone floor twenty feet below.

He took a deep breath, and braced his feet against the sides of the shaft.

*Help me, Lady...*he prayed to the goddess.

Slipping his hands under Allysian's arms, he began to pull her upward. The prisoners on the top tier tried to help by pushing from beneath, but he didn't dare watch, closing his eyes and beginning to inch backward. He felt as if his arms were separating from his shoulders as he supported her full weight for one heart-stopping moment. Giving one last mighty heave, Digan felt her hands grab hold of his tunic and pull as Allysian clawed her way up and over him.

"We did it!" she crowed, throwing her arms around his neck.

Digan hugged her back on instinct, and then loosed his hold as if burned.

I mustn't. I don't have the right... She is a princess royal; I am a penniless orphan—I must keep reminding myself of that fact. She was foolish to come after me, but I cannot compound that foolishness by taking advantage of her trust.

I must take her home. Vasileios will be beside himself with worry. I can't change that, but I can alleviate any further suffering. And then I will be off again. Trying to find somewhere to fit in...

It's too bad about the lute. After all the trouble gone through to get it, Talthos' refusal cuts deep, but there is nothing to be done about it now. The girl in the forest told me to stand up for myself, and I couldn't even accomplish that much. Just another one of my failures...

"Digan? What is it?"

"Just thinking." He smiled at her. "I know it's rare—but it's nothing to be overly concerned about. Come on. We must get out of here. This is no place for you, my lady."

Allysian began to crawl up the passageway. Digan was at her heels. The initial slope soon rose straight up into a vertical chimney. "Damnation..." Allysian breathed.

That was mild compared to what Mordigan wanted to say. His dread of heights was intensifying by the moment. Even the climb up the rain-slick cliff hadn't loomed so fearsomely before him.

The shaft rose for twenty-five or thirty feet. There was still no direct light at the top of the shaft, so it was not the end of the tunnel.

If one of us falls from the chimney, Digan mused, *they will hit the sloped shaft and slide out the opening in the ceiling. There will be no way to catch oneself. There is no choice, however. There is no other way out of the prison.*

"I'll go first," Allysian volunteered. She looked at him, a curious frown on her face. "Are you all right?"

"Fine," he coughed, the lie sticking in his throat. "I'll wait until you are safe so that I can catch you if you slip." *Or at least try,* he thought with grim determination.

"Right." She braced her feet against one side of the shaft opening, and pushed up with her hands. She began to inch her way up the chimney with awkward care—it was not a skill commonly required at the palace, but she managed it with fair success. Reaching the crest of the shaft, she slid backward into the opening at the top, and then peered down at him over the edge. "It's another section of slope, Digan, and then one more shaft...but I can see light at the top of that. We're almost free!"

It was easy for her to say. He looked up at the shaft looming above him. Digan took a deep breath and began to climb. Inch by inch he made his way up the shaft.

Just as he was getting his confidence back, his foot slipped, and he dropped several inches before catching himself, scraping half the skin off the palms of his hands.

By the Harp, that was close...

His heart skittered painfully in his chest, and he waited until he could get his breathing back under control before he started forward again.

When at last he slid over the edge of the shaft he lay on his back for a moment, trembling from the narrow escape. Allysian looked down at him with that same curious expression. "Are you really all right?"

"I'm fine, I tell you—" A spasm of coughing shook him, and he rolled onto his side, trying to fight down the panic as the lie burned through him like fire.

"You are not all right. What is wrong?"

Rising to his knees in the low tunnel, he murmured, "I'm afraid of heights," the admission sour in his throat.

Allysian knelt beside him, placing a gentle hand on his arm. Her hands were big for a girl, with square, capable fingers. "Why didn't you tell me?"

"What difference would it make? There was no other way out of the cell—unless you think we should go back and try to take out those guards. Shall we keep moving?"

"Let's rest here for a moment. I'm rather tired myself..."

Digan studied her in the dim light from the shaft above them. She was very delicate...her thin face intense beneath the uneven frame of her raggedly trimmed hair. Though fifteen, she was still boyish in build, with slim hips and a tapered waist. She was thinner than when he saw her last...

Her mouth quirked in a half-smile. "Are you finished?" she asked, laughter bubbling beneath the surface of her voice.

"W-what?" He was startled out of his reverie.

"Are you finished staring at me?"

Mordigan felt the blood rushing to his cheeks. "I-I'm sorry—I didn't mean to stare. It's just—"

She cocked her head expectantly.

"—You are so beautiful," he breathed, without stopping to think.

Allysian covered her mouth with her hands to stifle her laughter. "People have always said you are a smooth-tongued liar, Mordigan Bryre—they look to be right."

"You have no reason to believe me, Your Highness...but I am not lying now." He dared not look at her again.

Digan crawled away from Allysian to the bottom of the final shaft. "I will go first this time. There may be guards above." He climbed to the top of the shaft without a second thought, too embarrassed by the exchange to think about the height of the chimney.

When he gained the top, he found that there was a fine mesh grate over the hole. His heart sank, but he placed his shoulder against it and pushed as best he could. It was difficult to get leverage at the awkward angle, but luckily, the grate was more to keep out debris than to provide a barrier. It was never conceived that anyone would try to escape in this fashion, and the grill moved aside with a dull thud.

Climbing out of the hole with caution, Digan glanced around him. The shaft came out some distance from the court building, at the top of a cliff overlooking the sea below. There was no sign of any outside sentries or patrols. Leaning back into the hole, he called softly, "It's safe, Highness." He reached down and helped her out of the shaft.

Replacing the grill to conceal their escape, the two fugitives stole away from the cliff. The ground was littered with stones, which cut through the thin soles of Digan's soft boots like they were paper. He winced, as he looked for a clear path for the princess, trying to spare her pain. The dim moonlight faded in and out of clouds that scuttled across the sky in ever increasing numbers. Summer was fast dying, and there was a warning hint of the coming winter in the rising breeze.

Mordigan shepherded the girl along, glancing over his shoulder in uneasy dread as they fled. *No matter which way I turn, I botch things up... I just hope that I am able to return Allysian to her father without further incident. At least I will have done one thing right in my life.*

CHAPTER 6

THE NIGHT SKY DANCED with lightning, thunder grumbling a sullen accompaniment, as the fugitives stole away from the cliff that housed their prison. Digan cast an anxious eye upward and urged Allysian onward, hoping against hope to find shelter before the threatened deluge descended.

If we have to trek through a storm, we'll both catch our deaths. I must get her somewhere safe.

The weeks of imprisonment were taking their toll on the princess, however, and she often stumbled over the uneven ground. He kept one hand on her elbow, helping her over the worst spots as best he could.

The travel itself was no effort for Digan, afoot for weeks now, but the ruins of his boots no longer gave much protection, and he gritted his teeth as he limped on.

There must be something. I must get Allysian under some sort of cover before the rain begins to fall.

But it was not to be. The lightning redoubled; thunder split the night with mighty whip-cracks of sound; and it began to rain—great lashing sheets of water that soaked them to the skin almost instantly. Digan wrapped his ragged, sodden cloak around the princess, but it didn't do much to help stop her chattering teeth. The silken ruins of his own shirt clung to him in clammy folds, and the waterlogged velvet of his tunic began to weigh heavily on his shoulders. He didn't know where he lost his cap...or even when, and the thick hair plastered to his head dripped rain into his eyes, making the way even more difficult to see, and stinging like attacking insects.

Digan never felt more miserable in his entire life.

But I can't let her see. I must keep her spirits up. She's been through enough. No sense in frightening her.

"You look like a drowned kitten," he teased, swiping the heavy wet strands of hair out of his own eyes with an ineffectual gesture.

"I suppose you think you look better?" she retorted, huddling deeper into the cloak and trying to stifle a sneeze.

"Bless you, my lady."

Allysian drew her wet sleeve across her face as the storm worsened. "I hate the rain. I'm cold, and wet, and I want a hot bath and dry sheets."

"This will teach you to run away from home," he chided.

"That's right! Next time I'll just let Fate do as She wills with you, Mordigan Bryre!" She was shouting to make herself heard over the now howling wind.

With an angry disgusted snarl, she turned, stalked away from him—and disappeared. There was a startled squawk, and she was gone.

"Allysian!" Digan yelled, running forward. He skidded to a stop at the lip of a sudden drop. A muddy stream rushed by some three feet below him, almost invisible in the dark. "Allysian! Answer me!" He could not control the tinge of panic in his voice.

The water swept by him with terrifying speed, and

he could make out only vague dark shapes bobbing in the current. Whether or not the princess was one of them was impossible to tell.

"Digan! Help—" The high, thin cry ended in an abrupt watery gurgle, and Mordigan fairly flew down the slippery bank.

He slid into the water with a splash, losing his footing and submerging in the icy stream. When he fought his way back to the surface, he thrashed clumsily to stay afloat.

Where is she? Oh, great Hathor, where is she?

The night was black beneath the roiling storm clouds, and the slashing curtain of rain further obscured his sight. He lost track of which way was the nearer bank. The stream could not be more than ten or twelve feet wide, but he could not get enough purchase on the slick bottom to stand, and he was a poor swimmer at best. "Allysian!" he cried out, fighting to keep his head above the water, "where are you?" His voice cracked in panic.

"Here... Digan...I can't—"

He dove toward the sound of her voice, and made out the pale gleam of her hair as it sank beneath the raging torrent.

By all that's holy, why must I earn only ill fortune? Can I have one bit of good luck? Please, Hathor!

He lunged, grabbed a handful of sodden cloak, and hauled upward.

Allysian's head broke the surface with a sputtering gasp, and she clung to him like a leech. Her panicked strength shoved him beneath the water without warning, and Digan gulped in a large quantity of filthy liquid.

His lungs were on fire as he fought to get his head above water level. The soggy velvet tunic was like a shirt of chainmail as it soaked up more and more of the stream, and tugged him deeper beneath the surface. He couldn't struggle free of the garment because Allysian's legs were wrapped tightly around his waist, both hands tangled in his hair.

Digan flailed out blindly and lucked upon a solid object, striking it with sufficient force to bruise the back of his hand. He grabbed onto it and pulled with all his remaining strength, slowly dragging them toward it. He jerked Allysian's hand out of his hair, sacrificing a large hank of the wet strands, and anchored her to the half-submerged tree trunk.

As the princess transferred her stranglehold to the tree, Digan could finally lift his head above the water, and he drew in great, whooping lungfuls of air. He threw his arms over the trunk and clung to its solid strength.

Thank you, Lady Hathor.

He rested his forehead on the rough bark.

"We've g-got to g-get out of t-the water," Allysian shouted in his ear.

Digan bobbed his head in acknowledgment, too tired to do more.

"Which w-way is the s-shore?"

"I can't tell," he rasped. "It's too dark—I'm all turned around."

"H-how could it b-be so c-cold in the middle of s-summer?" The girl's teeth were once again chattering so that she could barely speak.

Reminding her that summer didn't stop merely

because she was locked in a dungeon would only scare her more. She'll realize it on her own in time.

"Try not to think about it," he soothed.

"Digan...I'm f-frightened."

"I know." Mordigan slipped an arm around her shoulders. "Don't worry. I'm here. Everything will be fine." The lie sent him into a fit of coughing.

"Are you all right?" Allysian asked, the anxious tone in her voice gladdening his heart despite their danger.

"I'm fine," he croaked, clearing his throat with a rough cough. "Can you pull yourself up onto the tree trunk? At least you'll be out of the water that way."

"I'll t-try." With a push from Digan, she managed to drape herself across the relative safety afforded by the trunk. "You c-come up too," she ordered, reaching out her hand.

Digan shook his head. "There isn't enough room for both of us. We'd both drown. I'll be all right. Dawn can't be too far off." He earnestly *hoped* that wasn't a lie.

Despite his efforts to stay awake and on guard, the cold water sapped his will, and his eyes slid shut.

No...I can't fall asleep. I have to guard the princess. I have to keep her safe. It is my fault that she is here. I must get her back to the palace where she belongs...

He forced his lids open for a time, but in the end, the effort was too great, and he drifted into the darkness, one arm hooked around a branch of the tree, the other hand clutched tightly in Allysian's grasp.

His thoughts wandered back along the path of his travels.

How beautiful the Azure City looked in the sunlight, with the crystal sparkling like sapphires...

but more beautiful yet are the streets of home. How I miss the chaos of a holiday in the Guild Hall...even Starsen sings better on a Feast Day. I could bear a dozen strikes from Cormeyer's cane with goodwill if it meant I was home. Home...

Allysian's startled exclamation brought him back to reality with a jerk. Unfortunately, in the confusion of the moment, he forgot where they were, and he almost drowned himself before he remembered to tread water.

The dull pearl of pre-dawn suffused the air, and they could see now why they became disoriented in the night. What once was a shallow stream at the bottom of a narrow defile was now part of a sheet of water spreading out around them in a placid lake. The dead tree to which they clung was the only solid object to be seen.

Digan swallowed hard, then pried his arm loose from the branch it curled around. "I will go and see if I can find a dry patch, Princess. You stay here."

"Oh, no you don't, Mordigan Bryre! You were in the water all night. You must be frozen stiff."

"It's not that bad," he lied—and felt a fire tongue in his throat to show the falsehood did not go unnoticed. He coughed and dipped a handful of water to soothe the ache.

"Don't drink that!" Allysian commanded. "It's filthy!"

"It's cool and it's wet," retorted Digan, his voice roughened by fatigue and exposure. "My throat feels like hot sand has been poured down it."

"I knew it! You'll be sick before the day is out. Climb up out of the water. It's my turn to be wet." She slid off of the tree trunk before he could offer further protest. "Ohh...it's still cold," she grimaced. "Get up there!"

"Allysian, please..." he began, "I can't let you—"

"Don't argue with me, Digan," she murmured, raising a gentle hand to his cheek. "You look terrible... and you're burning up! You've got a fever. Please get out of the water. I can't make it home without you, Digan—and I don't really think I want to try."

"Compromise? We'll go together." He stepped away from the tree, and almost slipped under the water again.

Allysian pushed him back against the trunk. "Digan, please listen to me. You're exhausted, and you're ill. You'll only make yourself worse if you won't be sensible. Just let me try—I promise I won't get hurt. I won't even leave your sight. It's my turn to rescue you."

Her arguments are true enough. I'm so cold I can scarcely feel my legs, but what I do feel aches all over. Besides, even if I don't want to let her have her way, there is no way I can stop her. I haven't the strength.

Digan nodded wearily and tried to pull himself out of the water onto the tree. He couldn't manage it.

Allysian slipped her arms around his waist and hugged him with all her strength her cheek pressing against his chest. "Don't die on me, Digan," she whispered. "Not when we've come so far..."

"I'll do my very best not to," he promised bemusedly, fighting down the urge to hug her back.

"That's right, you will!" With a flash of dazzling smile, she pushed away from the tree and swam away, cutting through the water with clean, even strokes.

She certainly didn't need me to rescue her, he thought, watching her steady progress. *Blind panic must have overcome her last night. She swims like a fish. One more thing she can do better than I can...*

Digan closed his eyes in apathetic defeat, slumping back against the tree. His head was spinning, and he felt like the half-hearted promise was already broken.

But I can't afford to be ill. Whether or not Allysian is capable of taking care of herself, it is my fault that she is out here on her own—in a foreign kingdom where she could very well be in greater danger than she realizes. I know many a tale of rival monarchies that used the children of a king as hostages of fortune against him. And she is so cursed sure of herself...

"Digan!"

He came to his senses to find Allysian shaking him violently. She was staring at him with a worried frown. He realized with dull surprise that only sheer luck kept his head above water as he slid down in his sleep. "What is it?" he mumbled, dazed and confused as he struggled to push himself upright.

The water was a good deal lower already. It rose only to Allysian's waist as she stood before him. "Can you walk?" she asked.

"I think so."

She slipped a hand around his waist and pulled his arm securely across her shoulders. "The shore is only a little way away now. We need to get you out of the water and dry. I found an old cabin about two or three hundred yards from here. When we get there, you're going to rest. No arguments."

He favored her with a shaky nod.

Even if I wanted to deny her anything, I don't have the strength.

Inch by painful inch, Digan managed to stumble to the cabin, grateful for her strong support. By the time they traveled the short distance, he was on his feet from stubborn will alone. His head was on fire, and whirling like a child's top.

Allysian shoved the door open and half-dragged him to a low bed-frame. The mattress was gone, but the crisscrossed leather straps that once supported it were still in place, and she helped him sit down on the edge of the rough webbing.

"We must get you out of those wet things, Digan." Allysian tugged at his sodden velvet tunic.

He caught her hands. "Princess— I'm all right. Let me..." He fell back upon the bed-frame, too weak to stay upright.

"Digan!"

"I'm all right...just let me—"

"You lie back and let me take care of you. I command you."

Digan tried to protest further as she stripped him of his wet tunic and shirt with efficient economy of motion, but he couldn't seem to keep his eyes in focus...

Allysian refused to give up on Digan. When she returned from her scouting expedition to find him in a semi-swoon, the ashen pallor of his tanned face frightened her nearly witless, but somehow she got him to the cabin. Now, she sat cross-legged on the floor beside the low cot, sponging his burning face with cool water as he tossed in a delirium of fever.

With his shirt off, she could count every rib. Always slender, Mordigan was now thin to the point of gaunt, and there were fresh bruises on his face and torso from his treatment at the hands of the Nausean guards. She traced the shape of the odd little scar just above his heart.

Where did you get this one, beloved? What adventures have you had in your wanderings while I waited in that dank cell?

There was another new scar running through his upper lip that she didn't recognize but thought she would have if it been there before. She ran a fingertip across it, feather-soft, heart hammering at the temerity of it.

What happened to you since I saw you last on the road outside of town? If I haven't exactly been living in comfort, at least I wasn't plagued with such violence. And where did you spend the past month?

Threadbare as his garments are, it wasn't on the streets of Nausa. He would have made his way into the dungeon long before this for vagrancy if he were going about looking so shabby!

She dampened his face with tender solicitude.

Digan muttered fretfully under his breath without ever coming fully conscious. "No...milady, I mustn't...he said unicorns were...I can't...Talthos...I don't understand...no, I promised...I mustn't break my promise..."

Allysian frowned. *I can't make any sense of it.*

"Allysian!" He cried out her name—in a tone so piteous and lost that she wanted to snatch him close and comfort him...but dared not.

She took his hand and held it tight. "I'm here, beloved. I'm here. I won't leave you. I promise."

The soothing words seemed to calm him, and he fell into an uneasy sleep.

Throughout the crisis of the fever, she knelt beside his bed, snatching a few minutes of sleep only when her eyes refused to obey her commands to stay open. Twice she thought she would lose him yet.

The first time, she grabbed his shoulders and shook him "Don't do this to me, Mordigan Bryre! Don't you do this. Please, Digan. Please!"

She scolded his unconscious form, dashing tears from her cheeks with the side of her hand. "You can't die on me. You can't leave me alone like this!"

He sighed softly, and the moment passed with a rally.

The second time, she threw herself across his limp body and cried until all her tears were spent.

He can't leave me now! What gods would be so cruel?

Finally, the fever broke, and the delirium was replaced with peaceful sleep. Allysian brushed the thick hair from his brow and planted a soft kiss in the center of it. In his sleep, Digan's lips curved into a sweet smile. The crisis was past at last.

Thanks to the Seven, Allysian breathed. She lay her head on her arm as she curled up beside his bed, and let her eyes close willingly for the first time in days.

Everything will be fine now. Digan will take charge again. He will take care of me. He always does.

She could rest now. Everything would be all right.

The next time Digan awoke, the sun was streaming down on the bed, and he lay beneath his cloak. His modesty was relieved to see that he also lay *within* his leggings.

At least Allysian didn't tried to go that far in removing my wet things.

His throat was parched, and his head felt like an empty bubble. *I am certainly glad it is attached to my neck...else I wouldn't be at all surprised to see it float away like a puff of cloud.*

Digan tried to push himself up on his elbows, but the attempt failed. He lay still, clutching at the webbing with both hands until the room stopped pitching.

"Don't try to move yet," Allysian cautioned, her quiet voice husky with fatigue. "You need to get your strength back. Here, drink this." She slipped an arm behind his shoulders and helped him to sit up enough to sip from the cup she held to his lips. "I was afraid I'd gone to all the trouble of cutting my hair and stealing these clothes for nothing," she teased, but her voice betrayed her as she continued in a whisper, "I thought I would lose you forever."

"How long?" he croaked.

"Two days."

Digan stared at her in disbelief. "Two days?"

"You were out of your head most of the time, moaning and muttering...mainly about things I didn't understand."

By the Harp, I hope I didn't say something I wasn't supposed to reveal...

"You're very brave," he commented softly, studying the shadows under her eyes with deep regret.

Allysian blushed. "No, I'm not. I cried my eyes out

when I thought I was going to be left here all alone."

"That doesn't mean you're not brave," he replied. "It just means you're human."

She flashed the half-smile that melted his heart like wax. "Well, I should hope so! If I'm not, why am I wasting my time on you?"

"Thank you, my lady."

"For what? And don't call me 'lady'! I told you about that—"

"For saving my life. And you *are* my lady—someday you will be my queen. You are a member of the Royal House, Allysian. I mustn't forget that...even if you want me to."

"Can't we just pretend...for now, at least...that I am just a girl, and you are just a boy...and that you love me back. At least a little?" Her voice trailed away into unhappy silence, and she bit her lip, staring down at her hands as they twisted together on the edge of the bed.

I wish I could lie to her. I would willingly accept the pain—no matter how great...but it wouldn't be fair to her. I mustn't let her dream...even if I long to share it with all my heart.

"I can't, Princess."

She buried her face in her hands so that she wouldn't have to look at him, and her words were muffled. "Forget...or love me?"

"Forget," he sighed, reaching out to touch the curve of her cheek with a hand that trembled despite his best efforts to control it. Her skin was damp beneath his fingertips. "I have to remind myself every moment of every day until you are home and safe."

Her shoulders straightened, and her hands came down. "I suppose I will have to accept that for now," she said, her voice brisk. Allysian swiped at her eyes and rose to her feet. "There's not a lot to eat, but it's better than nothing. You must be starved. Your clothes are pretty well ruined, but there aren't any others, so you'll have to make do." She handed him his shirt and tunic, keeping up a steady stream of inconsequential small talk as he shrugged into his garments.

Carefully, Digan swung his legs over the side of the bed and took a deep breath. Before he could even try to stand, she was beside him once more. "Let me help," she ordered.

"Aren't you getting tired of walking me around?" He leaned against her, grateful for her slim strength.

"I don't mind," she replied, with a shy duck of her head. She sat him down at a rickety table in the center of the cabin. "I hope you like fruit and nuts... there wasn't any way to start a fire, and besides...I couldn't catch any fish." She placed a trencher full of berries and nuts in front of him, and he wolfed them down. It was almost three days since the shared bowl of stew in the dungeon.

She sank down on a stool beside him. "Do you know when I first fell in love with you?" she murmured, tracing a pattern on the tabletop. "I've been thinking about this a lot over the last few days, and I think I've figured out the exact moment. Can you guess?"

Digan shook his head in denial, his mouth full of berries. *I'm not entirely sure I want to hear the answer to that question...*

"I was five. Master Cormeyer brought you to sing for my father. You were his pride and joy. Seven years old, with the voice of an angel. You stood up there, so proud and tall, and I sat on the floor behind Father's throne and peeked out at you from behind the cushions. Your song was the most beautiful thing I had ever heard in my life...and when you were finished, you caught me staring—and you winked at me. I fell in love with you right then."

Digan forgot to swallow. *Ten years? How could I fail to realize the depth of her feelings for ten years? Of course, she is the princess, and it would have been more surprising if I did consider the possibility that she noticed me. How strange to think that all the time I thought she was merely a sweet child, she fancied herself in love with me. And now that I...*

"I even started my lessons on the lute so that I would be able to come to the Hall at least once a week—"

"The lute!" Digan cried, bounding to his feet. He caught himself on the edge of the table as the room swayed before him.

Allysian moved to steady him. "It was hardly that exciting a revelation," she remarked, her tone dry with irony.

"No—Allysian, you don't understand—my... damnation." He fell back into the chair, his spinning head cradled in his hands. "My lute...I have to get my lute! I can't let him win...I can't. I have to go back," he finished, voice dull.

That much I remember from the delirium—the unwavering certainty that I must confront Talthos and make him honor his promise. I cannot ignore that unfinished business.

"Back where? To Nausa?"

He shook his head. "No. To the Azure City. To—I-I can't say any more."

"The Azure City? What are you talking about, Digan? Do you still have a fever?" Her hand went to his forehead, cool and soothing against his skin.

Digan brushed her hand aside with a petulant shrug. "I can't go home without it, Allysian. It is the only chance I have of proving to Master Cormeyer that I am not a complete failure. That lute—"

She twined her arms about his neck, and laid her cheek against his hair. "If you want this lute, then we will go and get it."

"I can't take you there. I couldn't ask you to risk the journey—it's too dangerous. But I can't go back until you are safe either."

What am I to do? My head is awhirl... But the Princess' safety is the main thing. I must take her back to Marineaux, and then I will corner Talthos.

"After I see you home to your father, I will go back and get it myself."

"I don't recall you asking me to do anything, Mordigan Bryre." She straightened and paced away from him with a stubborn frown, her arms folded across her chest in the imperious manner he knew so well. "I do as I please. I am a princess—remember?"

If there were any last, lingering doubts about the depth of my own feelings, the sight of her set face, eyes sparkling with angry tears dispels them all. I am hopelessly, and eternally, in love with this girl. She can never be mine, but even when I am old and gray, bouncing my grandchildren on my knee, Allysian will own my heart.

He gulped. "Aye, Princess. I remember." *And because I remember, I must never allow myself to tell her the truth.*

"Well don't just sit there staring at me," she snapped. "If you insist that you're going to be stupid and go gallivanting about by yourself, then you better take me home at once so you can come back and get this silly lute of yours. You'll probably go and get yourself killed in the bargain, but I know better than to hope that you will be sensible about the matter, so I suppose we better get started for home. What are you staring at me for?"

His newly laid resolve wavered. "You're a marvelous girl, Allysian."

She dashed away a tear that slipped past her iron control, commenting in a waspish voice, "Yes, yes—I know, and you think I'm beautiful, and brave, and a good sport...but I am too far above your station, so you could never, ever possibly love me—" She turned away with a sob.

I cannot leave her hurting so after all she did for me. Sensible or not, she deserves the full truth. I will deal with the consequences when they come.

Digan moved with slow care to her side, placing a tentative hand on her shoulder and easing her around to face him. He tilted her chin upward and gazed down into those beloved blue eyes, stormy with tears. "I know that I have no *right* to love you... that's the difference between us. It isn't that I *couldn't* love you...Sian—" he said, his voice like dark velvet. "It isn't even that I *don't* love you—"

Hope blossomed on her thin features. "You mean?"

Mordigan smiled down at her, his heart swelling with emotion. He ran his thumb across her cheek, gently brushing away the tears. "How could I not, beloved? But Allysian…"

She placed a finger on his lips. "No. Don't say any more. If there is even a chance that you love me, everything will be fine. Everything will be fine." She caught her breath and stood on tiptoe, winding her arms around his neck once more. "Would you please kiss me, Mordigan Bryre?" she murmured, her voice a mere whisper of sound. "You may consider it a royal command if you like…"

Heart thundering wildly in his chest, he bent his head to meet hers. The kiss was soft and sweet, and his soul sang within him.

Being here, now, with her, is a crime that could get me hung, but I don't care. For this one moment, she is mine, and I am hers. No one will ever be able to take this one precious moment away from us.

He let himself forget the probable consequences for now. Regrets belonged to the future.

Allysian broke the kiss to murmur, "Now, about this lute of yours…"

"It will still be there tomorrow," he replied, chuckling low in his throat. "Right now, I'm in the middle of a Command Performance."

She laughed in return. "That's right, you are. And I expect it to be the best performance you've ever executed."

"I will do my best, my lady," Digan promised. And he proceeded to try.

CHAPTER 7

LONG AFTER ALLYSIAN FELL into a well-deserved sleep, Digan sat outside on the rickety porch of the cabin, staring up at the cold, indifferent stars. His chin resting on his fists, he invented and discarded a thousand arguments he could use to persuade Talthos to live up to his share of their agreement. Toward dawn, he lost hope. There was simply no reason for the powerful wizard to comply with a homeless boy's hotheaded demands that he fulfill a bargain he did not want to enter into in the first place.

As the sun broke the horizon, Digan came to a decision. *I might as well accept the fact that I lost. After all the trials I went through to win the prize, in the end my efforts were in vain, and there is nothing to be done about it.*

Digan ran his fingers through his hair in a distracted gesture. There was a more crucial matter to deal with—he must ensure Allysian's safe return to her father. That was the only thing that was truly important.

He would simply have to live with the fact that he would never become a master bard. If he were lucky, he might be allowed to play for street fairs upon a borrowed lute as an unpaid background musician, but he would never command an instrument like the beauties Talthos crafted. He really *was* a failure...

With a wistful sigh, he bit his lip, watching the sunrise paint the sky with brilliant swathes of color. The composer within him yearned for strings beneath his fingers once again. He began to hum under his breath, trying to capture the melody he heard in his head.

The door of the cabin opened, and Allysian came out and sank down on the step beside him. "What's wrong?" asked the princess softly.

"Nothing," he murmured, ignoring the brief twinge of pain as he turned to her with a half-hearted smile. "Are you ready to go home and face your father?"

"Wouldn't it be more practical to go and get this lute of yours first? It is on the way back to Marineaux, isn't it?"

"The lute isn't important to me anymore." The enormity of this lie grabbed his throat and squeezed hard. A wracking cough doubled Digan over as he fought to breathe.

She put her arms around him and held him until the spasm eased. "I wish you would talk to me, Digan..."

"I...can't..." he choked out, shaking his head. "Please, Allysian, don't ask me to say any more."

Allysian pulled away from him, hugging her knees. "All right, Mordigan Bryre," she said, her voice stiff and formal. "Whatever you say. If you don't trust me, so be it." The frost in her voice cut to his soul.

Damnation. I've hurt her feelings. It is the last thing in the world I intended to do.

He rose to his feet with a sigh, not daring to face her. "I-I must get you home, my lady," he replied, his voice hushed. "The king will be beside himself with worry... Are you ready to leave?"

She shrugged. "I suppose so. It isn't as if I have a mountain of baggage. I will only be a moment." She turned and stepped into the cabin, slamming the door behind her.

Digan smacked his hand into one of the pillars supporting the porch.

Why can't I do even one *thing right? It isn't as if I am withholding the information from her by choice. I* want *to tell her about it. By the goddess, I long to tell her everything: about the crystal city, and the unicorn, and the wolf-girl...well, maybe not about the wolf-girl...*

But Freitanya promised terrible consequences for such a confession. And he did not dare make up a convenient lie—even the thought of losing his voice forever terrified him.

How could I afford to pay that fearful cost? Even for Allysian?

Allysian stiffened at Digan's evasion.

Just when I begin to hope he might return my feelings, he closes himself off from me again. Pushes me away with his words even as he pretends to love me.

She could see that her withdrawal hurt him, but she didn't care. He hurt her first, and she wanted to repay the favor.

There was no real reason to retrieve anything from the cabin, but she felt the angry tears pricking behind her eyes, and she was not about to let him see that he was making her cry—again.

She stalked about the tiny interior, throwing things from one place to another in a fit of temper. She got a great deal of satisfaction from the resounding crash the wooden trencher made as it split in two against the wall. The act vented the last of her frustration, and she glanced about the room for something to take with her to justify her trip inside the cabin.

There was still a little fruit left, and she bundled it together in an old square of cloth she found in the back of a cupboard. To her astonishment, she also found a set of shepherd's pipes wedged into the corner of it. Sitting cross-legged on the floor, she pulled them out and stared at them in dull surprise.

I searched every inch of this cabin while Digan was ill, and these pipes were not in that cupboard. I would swear to that fact.

A prickle of fear ran up her spine, but she shrugged it off.

I was rather distracted at the time. I must have overlooked the pipes, but they seem harmless enough.

She started to replace the pipes in the cupboard, but reconsidered.

This can never take the place of that lute Digan is pining over, but maybe it can serve as a kind of peace offering.

She slipped the pipes into her belt and picked up her bundle of fruit. She glanced around the cabin one last time.

It is strange, but I was happy here. Even when Digan lay so close to death, and I was afraid I would lose him forever, I felt a kind of contentment that we were together—alone and equal—whatever the outcome.

Now he will carry me back to the palace, where I will once again be a princess, and too high in rank for the attentions of a disgraced apprentice. It hurts to think he worries about such things, and yet I know it is my reputation he cares for. He has my best interests at heart, but I devoutly wish that for once he would be selfish instead of noble and self-sacrificing.

She stepped back out onto the porch, opening the door so softly that he didn't hear her. She stood for a moment, drinking in the sight of him. He leaned against a tree, his back to the cabin. His slumped stance painted a portrait of dejection, and his eyes were fixed on the far horizon. She could only see a portion of his face, but that portion was grave and still. He looked years older than on the day he was sent away from the Hall...and infinitely tired.

I wish I understood what brought that wistful sorrow to his face so that I could smooth it all away, but I know he will never tell me. Digan has always kept his emotions deep inside him, and now he is even worse.

Allysian sighed.

I can't stay angry with him. I love him far too much. And I know it isn't from choice that he will return me to Papa. It is just...he faced so much to rescue me from one prison only to force me back into another.

Digan heard Allysian's step behind him, and squared his shoulders.

I mustn't let her see me this way. There is no reason to burden her with my failures. I must be strong for her sake.

He pasted a smile upon his face, and turned to the princess. "Are you ready, Highness? We have quite a way to go yet."

"I'm ready," the girl whispered, eyes downcast.

She seems to be over her anger, but this quiet acceptance hurts even worse. What can I say to her? How can I heal that pain?

She handed him something she took from her belt. "I found this in the cabinet. I thought perhaps it might be better than nothing."

He looked down at the object in surprise. It was a fine set of shepherd's pipes. He blew an experimental trill on the instrument. The pitch was sweet and true. "They are wonderful, Sian—Your Highness. Thank you."

He saw the spasm of bewildered hurt that swept her face when he corrected his form of address, but hardened his heart against it.

I should never have allowed myself to call her anything else. And the memory of the kisses we shared is best forgotten. By the goddess, I was a fool to give in to my heart.

He would see her home safely, and then he would leave the kingdom forever.

It would be far too painful to stay and know that I can never hold her in my arms again. That moment was a precious gift, but it is gone, and it will never come again.

"We should go," he said aloud, suiting action to words by turning his back on the cabin. She followed him, wrapped in silence and the ragged remains of his cloak.

Though the sunlight was clear and bright around them, the summer was definitely gone. Digan shivered in his thin silk shirt. There was a distinct chill in the air, and the fields that had been lush and green when he passed them last were now golden with ripened crops ready for harvest.

So much time has passed... Vasileios will have sent troops far and wide, scouring the countryside for his missing daughter. Does the king know she ran away of her own free will?

Digan froze as a thought struck him.

Allysian ran into him. "What—Digan, you are white as a dove. What's wrong?"

"Sian," he asked, forgetting his resolve to be formal in the extremity of the moment, "what did you say to your father before you left?" His voice vibrated with urgency.

"Nothing."

He grabbed her by the shoulders and gave her a little shake. "Think!" he ordered, his fingers tightening. "Did you speak to him at all that day?"

Allysian winced. "Digan...you're hurting me."

He dropped his hands and stepped back. "Please. It's important that you remember exactly what you said."

"I told him the same thing that I told you in the dungeon—that Master Cormeyer was unfair to send you away like that, and he must do something about it. He said it was Master Cormeyer's decision and sent me to my room. I could see he wasn't going to do anything about it so I didn't bother to speak to him again. I went to the Hall and...borrowed your clothes. Then I went back, cut my hair, and left."

"Did you leave a note? Tell a servant where you were going? Anything?"

She shook her head. "No. Why?"

Digan sank onto a nearby rock, his head in his hands.

"Digan—what is wrong?"

He looked up at her, too crushed to be gentle. "Don't you see, Allysian? There is nothing to prove that you left the palace alone and of your own free will. With my reputation, your father probably

believes that I persuaded you to run away with me—
or worse yet, abducted you bodily."

"The page boy who let me into your chamber—"

"—Is a mere child, and will say whatever he feels
is wanted of him in order to avoid a beating. I can't
say that I blame him for that. Master has a heavy
hand at times."

Allysian crouched down before him, one hand on
his knee. "What does it matter, Digan? When I tell
Father what happened—"

He took her hand, and smiled down at her. "You're
right, Princess," he began, forcing a light tone into his
words. *There is no need to frighten her with the truth.*

"I'm sure everything will be fine." He managed to
stifle the cough that rose to choke him as he stood
and lifted her to her feet. The next words came out
smoothly, to his great relief. "I will see you back
to your father by tomorrow night," he promised.
"Come, we must move on."

When he would have let go of her hand, she clung
to his with surprising strength. He gave in with a
crooked smile, and they traveled on, hand in hand.

The weary hikers finally made it to the Marineaux
border at twilight the next day. It was still a good two
hours walk into the capital, but their spirits rose with
the thought of home, and their steps were light as
they hurried forward. It was only when they reached
the edges of the city itself that Digan stopped, a
stricken expression shadowing his thin face.

Allysian laid an anxious hand on his arm. "What
is it, Digan? We're almost home. Everything will be
all right now."

"I had let myself forget for a little while...but I-I have no home," he stammered. "I don't know where to go from here. I cannot go to the Hall without Master's permission, and I have never known any other place. There is no one to ask for shelter..."

"You will come to the palace with me then," Allysian stated, in a firm, no-nonsense voice, taking his hand in hers once more.

He hung back, resisting her deceptively light grip. "I can't do that Allysian! Your father will want my head as it is."

"Don't be silly," she scoffed, dragging him along with her.

Digan didn't want to hurt her any further, and so he went...but he knew better than to hope her naiveté would be borne out.

Vasileios will be in a killing rage when he sees his daughter. Allysian is filthy, bruised and thin as a reed. Those clothes are mere rags, and her eyes—oh, Hathor—those smudges underneath them look like she's been beaten...it will do no good to mention that she earned them in the sleepless nights she spent beside my sickbed.

Digan knew he didn't look much better, but doubted that fact would move the king. The thought that struck him on the road returned with painful certainty as he gazed down at Allysian's earnest little face.

Someone is going to be held responsible for this escapade—and I swear by all I hold holy that it will not be the princess.

So he let himself be led, faster and faster as they drew nearer to the palace, until she was dragging him along at a run. Allysian's expression of eager anticipation broke Digan's heart.

I fear she will be sadly disappointed in the king's reaction to her homecoming.

Just outside the palace walls, Digan stopped, refusing to go any further.

Allysian looked up at him with a puzzled frown.

He raised a hand to touch the girl's cheek. "You are home safe now, my lady Allysian. Go in to your father. He will be overjoyed to see you."

Allysian stared at him, her eyes wary. "Digan..."

"Go on—everything will be fine now, Princess," he promised with a shrug, fighting back the cough.

"You talk as if you were leaving me here. You can't, Mordigan Bryre. You can't leave me alone!"

"Allysian...Sian...I—"

"No! Digan, please!" The cry tore at his heart, but he steeled himself to defy her.

"It is for the best, my lady."

"I command you—"

"—To stay?" he murmured. "If you truly so command me, of course I will obey you, Princess... but you *do* realize that your father will have me hung for this escapade?"

It was cruel of him to phrase it so bluntly, but from the ashen expression that transformed her face, it was obvious that she *hadn't* realized it.

"No...no, you are right. You must leave at once. They can't find you here! Oh, Digan," she sobbed, clinging to him with all her thin strength, "why do I have to be a princess? Can't I just be a simple, ordinary girl?" She buried her face against his shoulder.

Digan chuckled low in his throat, lifting her chin, and looking deep into her tear-filled eyes. It struck him how they had stood in just these positions before, at the beginning of this great adventure.

How long ago that seems...and how very much both of us have changed since.

"You—my dearest Allysian—could never be ordinary if you tried. You are the most marvelous, eccentric, exasperating woman I have ever met, and I love you with all my heart." He kissed the tip of her upturned nose. "Believe that I will never stop loving you if I live to be a hundred. But you must go inside the palace now, and I—I must go somewhere where I can earn my own way."

"Where will you go, Digan?" Allysian moaned. "When will you come back to me?"

"Perhaps someday I will be able to redeem myself in my master's eyes, and time may well placate your father's wrath. If I can come back to the city in the future, I swear I will do so...but for now, it would be best for you to try and forget—"

"Never!"

"Even if I do come back, Allysian, things can never be the way you want them to be. You do know that, don't you?"

"Why not?" she replied, with the stubborn set to her chin that he loved so well.

"Oh, my dearest girl..." He hugged her to him, resting his cheek in her soft hair. "How I wish we could live in your world," he murmured, wanting with all his heart to give in to her pleas, but knowing the reality was not so simple. "But it doesn't exist. You are a princess...and I—I am a commoner, and a shiftless liar at that."

"But you're not, Digan—not anymore!"

"Though easily earned, such a reputation is difficult to shed. No one would ever believe I was telling the truth, Allysian. No one but you."

"Why isn't that enough for you?" she persisted, voice choked with emotion, tears streaking her grimy cheeks.

He set her away from him, tucking a strand of hair behind her ear with a tender caress as he gazed into her eyes in the growing gloom. "My darling girl, do you really want me to stay? Say the word, and I will do so—let your father's soldiers do as they wish..."

"No. You're right. You must go." She swiped at her face with a clumsy hand. Then she took a deep, ragged breath and smiled up at him with false cheerfulness. "I'll be fine now. Thank you for...for seeing me home." It was all she could manage. With a strangled sob, she turned and fled toward the palace.

He watched her go, aching with longing. *She will be safe now.*

He saw a square of light stream out across the grounds as she entered, and even from his remote position could hear the startled cries of welcoming inquiry. "Goodbye, Allysian..." he whispered.

Turning to leave, Digan found himself staring at a pair of liveried sentries. His heart plummeted into his boots, and he took a step back.

"Well, well. What do we have here?" asked one of the guardsmen in a growling purr.

"Why, I do believe we have us a fugitive from justice," replied the other, with a wicked grin. "What do you think the king will say when he sees this prize?"

Digan didn't wait to find out.

He ran for his life, dodging an outstretched hand to slip past the guards and into the warren of streets beyond. His idle loafing in the marketplace and surrounding environs served him well now. He knew the maze of alleyways and back streets like the strings of his lute, and he soon left the guards far behind.

He didn't dare stop running until he was deep inside the city, far from the palace. Finally, a stitch in his side forced him to rest, gasping for breath against the side of a building in the poorest quarter of town.

That settles it, he thought, with a rueful shake of his head. *King Vasileios blames me for Allysian's disappearance—just as I expected. Every guardsman in town will be looking for me now. The sooner I am out of the capital, the better for us both.*

He was far too well known here; his tall, slender figure a familiar sight on the streets of the city. There was nowhere for him to hide. If he stayed, capture was inevitable.

He sank to the ground at the base of the wall, head bowed between raised knees. *By the goddess, how I ruined things...*

A slight scrape of leather on stone propelled Digan to his feet in an instant, back pressed to the wall, fists clenched before him.

A semi-circle of ragged figures surrounded him, leering and menacing by turns.

"Look what we have here, boys," chortled the leader of the scruffy band.

Digan's heart skipped a beat as the circle began to close.

Allysian sat on a footstool before Vasileios' throne; cheek resting against her father's knee as he stroked her freshly washed hair.

It feels so good to be home, and fed, and safe...there is only one thing missing to make this happiness complete. Surely Papa can persuade Master Cormeyer to forgive Digan. I know he was worrying unnecessarily...I am positive Papa can put everything back the way it was before. Digan could return to the Hall, and in time, who knows what I can persuade him to accept?

She straightened, and twisted around on her stool to face Vasileios. "Papa—"

"Yes, my darling girl?" Vasileios smiled tenderly, an expression of incredulous wonder in his eyes. It was as if he still could not believe that she was real.

The endearment forced her to swallow hard before replying. "About Mordigan Bryre—"

His expression hardened. "We will not speak of him. When he is found, he will be dealt with. You need not fear that villain again."

"But, Papa, that's what I want to speak to you about. You have it all wrong. Digan is no villain—"

"No more, Allysian. Forget the name of Mordigan Bryre. He will soon be as dead to the world as he is to you now."

The very thought made her senses reel. "What are you saying?" she whispered faintly.

"There is a price on his head. He will not escape justice for long."

"But he has done nothing wrong!"

Vasileios cupped her cheek in his hand. "My precious child, you have such a generous, good-hearted nature that you are willing to forgive your tormentor all—I am not so charitable. Mordigan Bryre will pay for every bruise on your sweet face, and the scars to your spirit that can never heal."

"But, Father—you must listen to me!" She took hold of both his hands, trembling with the urgent need to make him hear what she was saying. "Digan did nothing wrong! He didn't even know I had gone after him. If it hadn't been for Digan, I—"

Vasileios pulled away from her and stood. "Enough, Allysian!" he ordered, his voice filling the chamber. "I will hear *no more* about it! The warrant is laid. If Mordigan Bryre shows his face again in my kingdom, his life is forfeit."

"But won't you at least—"

"You are tired, my dear. Go to bed." Although couched in sympathetic terms, there was no question that the statement was an order.

And Papa will entertain no further discussion on the subject...

Eyes blurred with tears, Allysian rose. "As you command, my lord king," she murmured, her voice a broken thread of sound. Bobbing an awkward curtsey, she stumbled from the room in a daze, hampered by the full skirts swirling about her feet. After nearly six weeks in the tunic and leggings of a boy, the gown was awkward and cumbersome.

Well, I will soon fix that.

She hurried to her bedchamber, and searched for the grimy garments she had removed to bathe.

I must warn Digan that his fears were justified. He must leave the kingdom at once.

The clothes were gone. It was a momentary setback.
I will just have to make do with my skirts.

Allysian ran back to the chamber door. It was locked.

"It can't be..." She stared down at the handle in disbelief, and then twisted it again, harder. The door was definitely locked.

She pounded on the door. "Dame Madeline. Open this door! I command you—"

"It is for your own safety, Your Highness," came a cool voice from the other side of the panel. "You've undergone quite an ordeal. You must rest."

"Let me out of here."

"Perhaps tomorrow, Allysian. For now, go to bed."

"I am not a child! You can't do this to me."

"You have acted as a child. Now you are reaping the consequences. Good night, Allysian."

"Please! They'll kill him—"

"Good night, Allysian."

She heard the click of retreating footsteps and felt her heart sink. Never before in her life had her way been barred within her own castle. The realization was devastating, but secondary to thoughts of Digan's peril.

Falling to her knees before the panel, she examined the keyhole. The key had been removed, so she couldn't even try and retrieve it.

It is a heavy door...I'll never be able to force it open.

She whirled, beginning to panic as she searched the room for an alternative.

Digan is in grave danger. I must go to him before it was too late.

She could see no other way out of the chamber. The narrow window openings were high and barred, and her dressing room only accessed the bedchamber. She was trapped.

Digan watched the circle of beggars, his expression wary, and his fists ready to strike. His weight rested on the balls of his feet, ready to cut and dodge if given half a chance.

I can hold my own against reasonable odds...but this is six to one, and three of them are larger than me. I must keep the wall at my back at all costs.

"Rest easy, lad," boomed one of the men, "we don't want to hurt you. We've got a message for you—from the king." The speaker was huge, dressed in patched scraps of leather and velvet, with an incongruous froth of dirty lace at his throat.

"That's what I'm afraid of," replied Digan, with a set smile. "Well, I want no message from the king. All I want is to be left in peace. I will leave Marineaux as soon as it is light, and never return." His throat tightened over the last statement, despite its truth, but he raised his chin in proud defiance and went on. "Give that message to Vasileios."

"Oh, you thought—" The big man burst into hearty laughter. "No, no...little songbird, we don't truck with Vasileios. We speak for the true king of Marineaux— him who rules the dark ways and secret places. He would like to speak to you, boy."

"I know only one king, and I serve Vasileios... even if he does want my head at the moment. So, I'll just be going now." Digan began to inch away along the wall.

One of the ruffians stepped up to bar his way. Another closed him in on the other side. The spokesman took a step closer, flattening his big hands against the wall on either side of Digan's head. His breath reeked of garlic and onions as he leaned in. "I don't think you heard me right, boy. I am not making a request, but delivering a command. The king will speak with you. You're worth a pretty penny to him. Vasileios has a call out for your head —and he don't care if it's breathing. Whether you come easy or not is up to you."

Digan gulped. Quick as a cat, he dove under the big man's arm, making a break for the open street. They were on him before he cleared the alleyway.

This time, however, he wasn't caught by surprise and pinned from behind. Digan fought like a madman, and two of the men were already out of the fray before a third suddenly uttered a surprised moan and collapsed to the damp cobblestones of the street in a crumpled heap.

The burly spokesman whirled around with a suspicious snarl, and a second sling-stone thudded into his shoulder. Howling with outraged pain, the big man made a grab for Digan. Stones continued to pelt the remaining beggars, falling with cool accuracy, and the youth did his best to aid his unseen benefactor with his fists, dancing back out of the ruffian's reach.

Finally, blood streaming down the side of his face from a sharp rock's kiss, the leader barked an order to his remaining men, and they took to their heels.

Digan slumped down on the damp pavement, nursing the knuckles of his right hand. "You might as well come out," he called in dull acceptance. "You'll get the whole reward now, I suppose."

"What! You mean the great Mordigan Bryre is surrendering to the likes of me?" The low-pitched call mocked Digan from the shadows of a nearby alleyway.

"With an aim like that I'm not likely to evade you, and I'm too tired to fight anymore. What are you waiting for? Let's just get the whole thing over with." Digan started to push himself off the ground, then froze as a slight shadow detached itself from the darkness and glided closer. He frowned, trying to make out his rescuer's identity. "Do I know you, boy?"

The newcomer cocked his head in the pale light given off by the rising moon. "Aye, Mordigan Bryre, though I doubt you'd remember. I'm not one of your fancy friends with their uppity ways...but you did me a good turn once."

Something about the tilt of the boy's head was familiar, and suddenly the memory came.

It was nearly two years gone since Digan caught Payter menacing a ragged urchin by holding his head under the water of the fountain in the square.

"Leave him be," Digan ordered, pulling Payter off his victim by the scruff of his neck.

"He pinched my purse, Mordigan Bryre. I got a right to reclaim my own."

"Oh, I see..." Digan drawled, glancing at the other boys who were crowding around to watch the show. "You must drown a boy a foot shorter and twenty pounds lighter to retrieve sixpence."

The villagers laughed at Payter's hot protests of injury.

Digan rolled his eyes. "Get out of here, bully, before I tan your hide for you. Torturing small children...does that make you a man?"

"I have a right!"

"You have a right to feel my foot up your backside if you don't slink away to your rathole!" Digan stepped toward Payter, fist raised.

Sullenly, Payter retreated from the scene, with angry scowls and mumbled threats of future retaliation. The incident was one of the chief causes of the bad blood between Digan and the shop-boy, who hated being thwarted—especially in front of his peers.

Digan turned to the victim, who stood dripping on the cobblestones. "Are you all right?"

"Aye."

"Did you take his purse?"

"Aye."

Digan bit back a smile. "That sort of thing can earn you a beating, you know."

"Aye. But coming home empty-handed earns me worse."

Digan's own purse was full of coppers from a day spent playing before the gaming den, and he pressed a handful of them into the child's hand. "Go on with you now. And, next time, pick your marks more wisely."

"I won't forget this, sir."

"Sir? Me?" Digan laughed. "I'm no gentleman. Now, be off. Payter is not above calling the watch, lad."

"I'll repay you for this kindness one day. See if I don't."

Digan waved away his gratitude. "Just be more careful."

The boy disappeared into the crowd, and Digan never saw him again.

Until now.

"It seems you pay your debts with uncanny timing," Digan smiled, rising to his feet and automatically dusting the seat of his leggings. "Now, it is I who owe you, my friend—?" He put a note of inquiry into his expressive voice as he held out a hand, and the other, after a momentary hesitation, shook it.

"Gauston Sayre...so they say," the boy offered, with an enigmatic shrug. "You must leave here at once. The Beggar King will not be the only one searching for you—or the only one to find you. I can show you a safe way out of town."

"The help would be most appreciated," Digan *admitted, suddenly so weary he could scarce keep himself upright. "I don't think I could even find my way to the Guild Hall at the moment without bungling into someone after my hide." He shivered in the cold night air. The threadbare silk shirt did little against the chill.*

"Here, take this." Gauston slipped out of the knee-length wool cloak he wore and handed it to Digan.

The older lad fastened it about his neck with a grateful nod. It hung only to his waist, but it cut the wind considerably. At a gesture from Gauston, Digan raised the hood to hide his features and followed the boy through the moonlit streets.

CHAPTER 8

GAUSTON THREADED THROUGH THE night-shrouded alleyways like a cat, and soon, despite a lifetime spent roaming the city, Digan was thoroughly lost.

"Where are...we...going?" he gasped, fighting to keep up with the little thief. He was exhausted. He and Allysian pushed themselves to the limit getting back to the capital, and he was still weak from the fever. "Please...slow down."

Gauston shook his head. "We can't afford to. You can rest soon, but as long as you are in the streets, your life is in danger." He moved on.

Digan gulped. "Is it as bad as that? I expected imprisonment..."

"Vasileios has a price of twenty gold on your head, Mordigan. He means to see you hang."

"Hang?" *I never really believed it would go that far. And how can I trust this little one not to claim that prize?*

Digan slowed his pace, edging further away from Gauston.

The little street urchin turned to him, fists loosely balled on his hips. "I gave you me word to help. Whether or not you believe I'll keep it is up to you, but being a thief ain't the same as being no liar. Now, I can show you a safe way out of the city, or leave you to the Fate. It's up to you."

Digan managed a weak grin. *What have I got left to lose?*

"Lead on, Gauston...with thanks."

The younger boy nodded sharply, and hurried on, leading Digan to a tight crevice hidden in a clump of thorn bushes. The thorns clutched at hair and skin, raking a thin line of blood from Digan's cheek, before they fought through into the mouth of a cramped cavern.

"This way." Gauston pointed to the back of the small chamber, where a narrow cut fed into a tunnel high enough to stand upright in.

Once inside the tunnel, the passageway led further into the depths of the earth. Gauston turned to Digan with a warning finger to his lips. "Don't say a word to anyone," the boy cautioned in a whisper. "Just follow me and we'll cut through as quickly as we can. This passageway will get us to the other side of the city without risking the Guard." He gave Digan a measured look. "Slump down a bit, and keep that hood pulled close."

Digan did as the boy suggested, cutting six inches off his height and wrapping the cloak about him like a second shadow. As they hurried on down the passage, the growing stench of ripe sewage permeated the tunnel.

Digan's gorge rose. *Thank Hathor my stomach's empty, or I would disgrace myself sure*, he thought sourly.

"How can you stand that stink?" he whispered, wrinkling his nose against the smell, and trying to breathe through his mouth as much as possible.

"You get used to it after a time," Gauston confided with a grin. Then admitted, "But it takes a while." He gestured around him with an expressive wave of his arms. "And it's worth the aggravation. There's safety in these tunnels beneath the streets. Eventually this passage merges with the sewers running beneath the capital. We can travel anywhere in the city through them.

"Did you know that most of today's cities were built over older settlements? There are sturdy stone passages and chambers like these honeycombing the entire continent. They are safe places, and easily claimed by us pickpockets and gamblers who live in the Shadow Kingdoms. What with the extra space that natural tunnels and caverns provide, we beggars and street gypsies live quite nice here beneath the ground."

The younger boy's thin face glowed in the dim light of widely spaced torches guttering on the tunnel walls, and Digan found himself smiling at the other's enthusiasm.

This underground world might be alien to me, but the passionate pride—that I understand.

Digan glanced around to make sure that he would not be overheard, then dared to venture, "You sound like you have a high claim here, friend Gauston."

With a shushing gesture, Gauston grinned. "Some say so," he replied with another enigmatic shrug. "We must go in full silence from here. We are about to skirt the throne room. We definitely don't want to be caught now."

With a nod to show his understanding, Digan pulled the edges of the hood together in front of his face and followed Gauston. They halted near the entrance to a large, roughly circular cavern hidden deep beneath the city. Innumerable tunnels radiated outward from it like the spokes of a wagon-wheel. The central chamber itself was piled high with chests and boxes. Braziers of sweet-smelling wood and spices sent their perfumed smoke curling about the rough ceiling. There was the dusky gleam of gold in the shadows as torchlight glinted from candlesticks and serving utensils, and the brighter spark of silver was a frequent accent.

Silken pillows were strewn throughout the room, and here and there bodies lounged upon them. Courtiers dressed in tattered silk and velvet left behind their workaday serge and homespun until next they sallied forth into the city above.

Digan was painfully aware that his own bedraggled finery fit seamlessly into the group of beggars. *Ah well, I will probably wind up in just such an enclave somewhere, if Vasileios' men don't catch me first.*

"This way," Gauston murmured in his ear, hugging the shadows of the walls to circle the chamber on a ledge of stone that ran around the room. Digan trailed the boy around the perimeter, but glanced around him as they moved, his curiosity fully engaged.

In the center of the chamber was a great gilded chair. Seated upon it, one boot propped up on a velvet footstool, was a big man with a thick, waving mane of golden hair. His narrow, handsome face was highlighted by penetrating, nut-brown eyes, and a wide, winsome grin only slightly marred by a missing front tooth.

He couldn't help it. Digan leaned over Gauston's shoulder and whispered, "Who is that?"

Gauston shushed him, but volunteered in a low murmur, "That is Burian Sayre—here he is king!" The smug gap-toothed grin accompanying the words was a mirror of the big man's smile, and suddenly

Gauston's evasive shrugs and proprietary air were explained. "Come on, let's go."

"I acknowledge only one king," Digan said tersely.

"Who wants to stretch your neck for you," scoffed the boy. "The more fool you. If I hadn't come along, you would have bungled your way into a rope about your neck. Is your king better than mine?" Gauston wheeled and continued forward, back stiff with anger.

Digan bit his lip. He hadn't intended to hurt the boy's feelings, and cursed himself for not realizing that his statement would have that effect. It was obvious that Gauston was a loyal supporter of his "king," whether Sayre was in truth his father or not. Digan hurried to catch the boy up, and laid a hand on Gauston's shoulder. "I'm sorry," Digan apologized in a soft, placating tone.

Gauston jerked free. "He's a good king," the boy growled, his tone defensive. He turned and met Digan's eye with his chin jutting at a defiant angle. "He takes care of...his people."

Digan nodded in acknowledgment of the unspoken rebuke, and followed the little thief meekly.

Halfway around the huge chamber, Gauston froze, shoving Digan back against the rock wall. "Damnation!" the little thief spat. "I was hoping for more time."

Below them, the burly rogue with the lace cravat was stumbling toward Sayre. He went down on one knee before the king.

"Have you got him, Jedrek?" asked Sayre, in a melodious baritone.

"No, my lord," growled his lieutenant. "We did have, but someone 'rescued' him. Someone who done this." He swept back the greasy hair from his forehead, revealing a lump visible even from their vantage point. "And this." He pointed to the cut on his cheek. "Knocked Hubert and Penn clean out he did. Only one I know with an aim like that, and you got to do something about that boy."

Beside him, Digan heard Gauston gasp, "I'm for it now..."

"I see," purred the king. "Gauston!" The roar seemed to shake the chamber, and the boy jumped. "Come down from your perch—and bring your companion."

"How did he?" Digan breathed.

"Don't ask," replied the little pickpocket miserably. "We'd best go down, before they come fetch us."

They made their way down to the floor and Gauston led Digan to the throne, bobbing a deep bow. "Yer Majesty..."

"Well, well, well...the man of the hour. King Vasileios has offered quite a handsome reward for your capture. And there you were, wandering about the streets for anyone to see. My...subjects...were merely trying to save your hide. Good heavens, boy! Do you fancy a rope about your neck? Whatever possessed you to show your face in this town again? Mere stupidity alone is not enough to account for such recklessness."

Digan reacted with the smoldering anger that always led him into trouble. "And I suppose stupidity is one attribute with which you are intimately familiar," he snarled.

There was a breathless silence. Jedrek's hand came down heavily on his shoulder, and Gauston reached for the dagger in his belt, his eyes glittering with fury.

Sayre leaned forward and laid a restraining hand on Gauston's arm, chuckling throatily. "Careful, Gauston—a tongue as sharp as that can cut as deep as your blade."

The king rose to his feet. He was half a head taller than the rangy Digan, and muscular were the boy was wiry. "Do you wish to challenge me, boy?" He laughed indulgently. "The more fool you if you try. I am Burian Sayre—here *I* am king."

"As I told your man—I acknowledge only one king."

"Who would see you hang. How noble you are. And you call *me* stupid." Sayre resumed his throne with a shake of his head. "You have involved yourself in a fascinating state of affairs, little man. What was a beggar boy like you doing running off with the errant princess in the first place? Did you really abscond with her in hopes of regaining your position? If so, 'twas a foolish notion."

The blood rushed to Digan's cheeks. *I have not sunk so far as beggary yet. Whatever may come in future.*

"I had nothing to do with it," he protested hotly. "She ran off on her own. I just brought her home safely, that's all."

"Oh, ho! I've wounded your pride, haven't I?" The gypsy king chuckled. "Ah, youth..." His eyes narrowed thoughtfully. "But there's more to it now, isn't there? Good gracious, boy, have you gone and—you have. That's a pretty cauldron of fish you've fallen into."

Digan stared at the ground. *The man is entirely too perceptive.*

"I don't know what you mean," he growled, but the statement ended in a ragged cough.

"I think you do. No. You're not stupid, boy. You are something infinitely worse. You are a romantic." Sayre shook his head with a sigh. "But you are safe here...for now. I suggest you get some rest. You look done in. Gauston will show you a place to sleep."

He turned to the little pickpocket. "Take him to the guest chambers. And then come back here. I want to talk to you."

Gauston's face blanched, but he nodded and took Digan's arm.

Digan started to protest, but a push from Jedrek nearly drove the boy to his knees, and he got the hint. With a meek nod of acquiescence, he followed Gauston from the chamber.

Once they were out of sight of the throne room, Gauston dropped his arm and slammed his fist into the rock wall. "I am Fate's fool, I am! He will tan me good for this."

"I'm sorry if I caused you trouble."

"No matter. I'm always in one scrape or another. Follow me."

Digan sighed. "What's the difference? Your cell or Vasileios'...either way, the result is like the same."

"Would you stop feeling sorry for yourself and come on? We have to hurry, before he sends Jedrek to check up on me."

"I don't understand."

"I said I'd show you the way out, didn't I? I keep me promises."

"But what about your—king?"

"I'll smooth it over with him in time. May cost a strip or two of hide." Gauston shrugged. "'Tis no matter."

"Gauston, how will I repay you?"

"You done me good. Now, it's my turn. Come on."

Gauston led him through what seemed like miles of twisting corridors and interconnected galleries. They saw Sayre's subjects everywhere, hurrying to and fro on their own business. Some carried loot under their arms; others shed their beggar's deformities as they strolled along comparing notes of the day's take. Whenever they passed a group of beggars, Gauston took Digan's arm and pretended to be shepherding him along.

Mordigan was impressed with their sheer numbers. *If Vasileios ever decides to take on the beggars, he will have quite a fight on his hands.*

"Up here," the smaller boy muttered at last, gesturing up a sloping walkway. A ragged exit at the top of the slope led out into the open night air.

Digan climbed the hill on legs that shook with the strain. *I don't have much more to give,* he thought dully. *I hope I can find somewhere to snatch a few hours sleep.*

He turned to Gauston with an outstretched hand. "Thank you again, Gauston. I owe you my life."

"We'll all be safer without you in the city," Gauston answered, his tone frank. "Vasileios is out for blood— and if he can't have yours, ours may do. As long as he knows you are free within his borders, the beggars and thieves will have to tread on eggshells. Fa—the King would have turned you over for immunity, you know. I can't let him make that mistake. But make sure you are seen far away from here. As soon as possible."

"I shall," Digan promised.

"Now, it won't take Jedrek long to realize I should have been back by now. He'll come looking for me. I can lie my way out of it by saying I was escorting you to the cell when you knocked me down and escaped. You're big enough that they may believe me—at least they won't be able to call the lie. This way leads to the road out of town. If you take it, you can be well gone by morning."

"Why are you taking such a risk to help me, Gauston? Is it really just because of Payter?"

"I don't want to see him hurt," the little thief admitted in a rough voice.

My heart has no doubt as to whom that "him" refers to. He swallowed hard at Gauston's fierce loyalty. *Hathor, how I envy this boy his relationship with his father—slight as it might be.*

"The only reason the king—the *real* king—leaves us alone is because he don't really want anything we have," Gauston continued. "You, he really wants. You ain't worth dying for."

Digan smiled ruefully at the sentiment, and the pugnacious way in which it was delivered. "I can't argue with you there, my friend. Here—" He handed Gauston the shepherd's pipes that kept him and the princess fine company on their journey home from the cabin. "They aren't much, but they're the only thing I've got. Perhaps you can garner a coin or two from them."

Gauston eyed the gift with a wary glance. "What are you giving them to me for?"

"Because you helped me."

"Mordigan Bryre ain't widely known for his charity. Or his good manners, come to that. You'd better look to your reputation."

"Perhaps Mordigan Bryre has learned a few things while he's been gone—and regrets the reputation he had earned..."

The smaller boy took the pipes. "Thank ye." He took a deep breath and visibly braced himself. "Now, hit me."

Digan stared at him. "I beg your pardon?"

"Come on, fool. Hit me. Do you think I can go back to *my* king without an excuse why you got away from me? He will know that the only way you could lose me is if you knocked me down, and I have to have the bruise to prove it. Hit me!"

Shaking his head, Digan pulled back his fist, and then hesitated. "I can't just hit you for no reason, Gauston—"

Gauston's own fist flew out and caught Digan squarely in the nose. Blinding pain roared through Digan's head, and he lashed out instinctively, striking Gauston in the jaw.

The little thief staggered back, flashing the gap-toothed grin that echoed Sayre's own with such suggestive resemblance. "Aye, that ought to do it," the younger boy nodded, working his jaw. "Good luck to you, Mordigan Bryre."

Gauston scampered off down the tunnel, and out of sight.

Digan stanched the blood flowing from his nose with the ragged cuff of his shirt. *What I wouldn't give for a nice, clean suit of clothing right now.*

I must get out of town, and reconsider my options. Perhaps I can coax another night's shelter from the woodcutter's wife. Her crops will be in need of harvest about now, and a willing pair of hands might well come in useful.

Digan stepped out of the tunnel into the chill night, peering with caution in all directions. It was only then he realized he still wore Gauston's cloak. He pulled it closer with a shiver.

I bet that the boy didn't forget I wore it. His charity just goes to prove that upbringing does not necessarily dictate behavior—that little thief showed far more consideration for others than this Hall-bred apprentice ever did.

With a disconsolate sigh, Digan started forward toward the road he could see beckoning before him. The stars glittering above his head in cold splendor never seemed so remote.

They remind me of...but then, everything does.

"There! That's him! Didn't I tell you?"

The cry tore the silence of the night, and Digan spun about, staring around him in wild panic. The voice was a familiar one—one he heard often in his nightmares since this whole affair began. It was Payter, crowing in triumph, and Digan saw the other now, clinging to a lamppost and pointing in his direction.

The sound of heavy movement around him broke Digan's momentary paralysis, and he ran for the road. It was too late. A full watch patrol cut him off, pikes in hand, and he froze. It was no use. He stared down the road, his heart yearning to be off upon it.

Escape was so close...but perhaps I knew all along that capture was inevitable. If not today, then surely it would be tomorrow. And I am so tired...

He raised his hands in a gesture of resignation, and let the guardsmen take him without resistance. As he was goaded toward the castle by the sharp prod of a pike in his back, his last sight of the clearing outside the beggars' cave featured Payter's victorious grin as he watched the guards lead Digan away.

Allysian teetered precariously on top of a chair balanced atop her dressing table, studying the barred slit of window in her bedchamber. It was still chest height to her, and about six inches narrower than she was. She was not all that deterred by this last problem, having decided that the loss of a bit of skin was worth it if she could get to Digan in time to make a difference. However, she wasn't quite strong enough to lever herself up onto the ledge, and there was nothing else she could stand upon.

The rest of the furniture is too heavy to move. But surely I must have something I can carry?

As she mulled over a way to alleviate this problem, there came the sound of a low whistle from the ground below. Curious, she stood on tiptoe and pulled herself up until she could just see the dim rectangle of yellow lamplight reflected on the grass beneath the tower. "Who is there?" she called in soft reply.

"My lady Allysian? Is that you?" The hushed voice was urgent, but she didn't recognize it.

She leaned out the window as far as she could, dangerously overbalancing on the flimsy chair. "Who is it?" she asked again.

"My name is Gauston Sayre. I bring news of Mordigan Bryre."

"What has happened?" Her panic made her voice louder than she intended, and the unseen speaker hushed her frantically.

"Quiet, please! I can't be found here. I just came to tell you—"

"What? What is it!" she broke in, impatient to hear his news, but taking care to keep her voice low.

"He's been captured, my lady. The guards led him away, and I fear he's in dire straits now. They were heading for the tower prison."

"I've got to get out of here! You, Gauston—show yourself. I can't see you from this angle."

A slight figure stepped into her line of sight, limned by the falling lamplight. Glancing warily from side to side, he peered up at the window, shading his eyes against the light from above. It was a boy, not more than twelve, and short for his age. "You've got to go to him, lady. Someone must help him."

"How can I help? I'm locked in my room."

Gauston measured the window with a calculating eye. "Stand back from the window, lady, and I'll come up. I can open the lock."

There was an element of professional pride and an unconscious arrogance in his voice that left her no doubt that he could do as he claimed. A thick tangle of ivy vines clung to the wall outside her tower, and Gauston scrambled up them like a sailor in the rigging of a familiar vessel.

Allysian watched him with a touch of envy. *I never would have been able to make it down so neatly.*

The boy slipped through the window with an easy grace and stopped dead on the windowsill, looking around the room in slack-jawed awe. The princess surveyed the chamber with a puzzled frown.

I've never really thought about how the gilt fixtures and velvet draperies must appear to an outsider. To me, it is simply furniture.

"The King could get a right fortune for this lot!" Gauston murmured under his breath.

"Why should he sell it?" asked Allysian in confusion.

Gauston stared at her, and then ducked his head to hide his giggles. He bobbed her a sketchy bow. "Begging your pardon, lady. I forgot myself. And to whom I was speaking." His speech was a little stilted, as if he were unaccustomed to using such courtesies.

"Never mind all that," Allysian replied, struggling to hide her impatience and failing. "What about Digan?"

Gauston's face clouded, and his voice was grave as he answered, "He was slipping out of town when the watch was alerted. He would have made it away clean, but Payter Fletcher ratted on him. Mordigan didn't even try to put up a fight...not that I blame him that—there were seven of them, and they with pikestaffs. I saw him surrounded and brought this way. Where else would they take him but to the tower prison? Oh, lady..."

The boy fell on one knee before her, "He's a good-hearted fellow, is Mordigan Bryre. He deserves better than he'll get from your father. The whole town knows the price the king set on his head for spiriting you off."

"But he didn't!" Allysian protested.

"I'm not the one in need of convincing, lady. Your father is out for blood, and no mistake."

"I must go to him! Can you really open this door?" She gestured to the stout oak panel, and Gauston hunkered down in front of it, eye level with the keyhole.

He pulled on his lower lip, his face thoughtful as he examined the mechanism. "I was hoping for something a mite more difficult," he sighed at last, rising to his feet. "This is hardly a challenge." Reaching into his belt pouch, he pulled out a little ring of odd-looking metal rods, each ending in a different shaped tip.

Allysian watched with interest as the boy inserted one of the rods into the lock. It slipped in, but the mechanism didn't turn. Gauston nodded to himself and sorted through the ring a second time, choosing another tool with a similar shape. This time, there was a soft click, and he turned to her with an engaging, gap-toothed grin. "There, you see!" he crowed, his voice triumphant.

He pushed the door open with a cautious hand, and peeked around it. "All clear," he advised her. "Can you get us to the tower without being caught?"

"I think so," she replied. "I *have* to, don't I?"

They slipped through the palace with the same expediency Gauston and Digan used when navigating the underworld. There was one bad moment when they started to cut through the throne room, and only just managed to avoid being seen by Vasileios who sat upon his great chair reading from a scroll of parchment.

"We'll have to go the long way around," sighed Allysian in irritation, chafing at the delay. "Whatever is Papa doing up? He's always abed by now."

"I'd rather not guess," replied Gauston, his face grim, and Allysian blanched—thinking of all the unpleasant reasons the king might be up so late.

None of them bodes well for Digan.

"Come on," she urged, leading the way down a roundabout path that carried them through a less formal section of the palace. As they passed through the sitting room, she scooped something up in passing.

"Here, now! That will only get in the way," Gauston protested.

"Never you mind," retorted the princess. "It's for Digan."

Gauston subsided, mumbling under his breath, "Blame foolish girls are."

Allysian ignored him, cradling her lute close to her chest so the strings wouldn't accidentally sound.

There was one more close call at the entrance to the tower cell corridor. A guard sat on duty beside the heavy iron-studded door, but an empty bottle lay at his feet, and his snores could be heard from their concealment halfway down the hall.

A warning finger to his lips, Gauston crept to the door and examined it with care. It was unlocked. There was no fear that the prisoners beyond it would elude the sentry even if they did manage to escape their cells. The two conspirators slipped inside the prison block, and Gauston posted himself at the top of the half-flight of stairs leading down to the dungeon.

"Aren't you coming?" Allysian whispered. "I can't open the door."

"I thought you might like a chance to talk to him alone first," replied the boy, ducking his head with an endearing shyness.

Allysian flashed him a radiant smile, and laid a grateful hand on his arm. Gauston blushed crimson, and the princess dropped an impulsive kiss on the boy's cheek. "Thank you."

"For what, lady?" Gauston asked, with a puzzled frown.

"For coming to tell me, and getting me in here."

"Go to him, lady."

Allysian looked down the corridor. "What do I say to him, Gauston? How could my father do something like this?"

"He is the king, lady."

"What kind of excuse is that?" she scoffed, irritated that he should take the king's side in this.

"It is not an excuse, lady. It is a responsibility."

She looked at him in surprise. "I never thought of it like that before," she acknowledged.

Gauston perched upon the top step of the stair. "Go to Mordigan," he repeated in a soft murmur. "He needs you now."

She could see the slumped form in a cell at the far end of the corridor. Digan looked so hopeless. "Let's just get him out of here, Gauston."

Gauston looked up at her with a troubled expression, and admitted. "I can't, lady. I can't open these locks."

"How do you know? You didn't look at them closely. You haven't even tried to pick one!"

"Lady, this is my business. I can't open these locks."

She bit her lip. *To come this far and not save Digan? It hurts almost too much to bear, and yet, how much greater the suffering he must be going through. I mustn't add to his burdens.*

Allysian straightened her shoulders and hid the lute behind her back. She pasted a smile on her face.

Somehow I will get Digan out of this. But for now, I will give what comfort I can.

CHAPTER 9

DIGAN SLUMPED ON THE hard stone cot, his head in his hands. *There is no question of what I must do. I cannot—will not—let Allysian accept the blame for her actions. Yes, her own headstrong willfulness brought her out after me, but having her anger the king by defending me will not turn Vasileios' wrath.*

He got to his feet and began to pace, actions following his restless thoughts.

It will only damage her bond with her father if she tries to justify what happened, and I know how much they mean to each other.

He envied her special relationship with her father as he did Gauston's with Sayre, having never known his own father, and he refused to not let her jeopardize that bond just to save him.

The outcome will be the same regardless. Vasileios' mind is already made up...nothing will change that. I am not going to let Allysian do something she will only regret later in life. It will be the hardest thing I've ever done...but I will lie.

With a rueful grin, Digan contemplated that decision—for the first time in his life, he would be lying for the *right* reasons, and it would cost him his voice. For this was no harmless little lie—this was one of those extreme falsehoods that Freitanya warned him about.

Digan moaned, sinking down on the bunk once more and covering face with hands. The one good thing in his life he could truly call his own was his voice. It was his only comfort as a boy, his only pleasure as an apprentice. His singing was the one constant in his chaotic world... but if he must give it up to save Allysian from herself—he would do it without a moment's hesitation.

Why? Because—also for the first time in my life—Mordigan Bryre truly loves something other than himself.

"Who would have thought?" he whispered. "Whoever would have thought?"

With a ragged sigh, he lay back on the hard stone bunk, shifting uncomfortably as he stared up at the ceiling of his cell. The bruises from his altercation with the beggars were supplemented by a host of new ones when the watch grabbed him. Now there was an additional crop of aches and pains to adjust to.

Not the least of which is my nose, he thought with a smile. *Not that I expect to have much time to worry about my bruises.*

He threw an arm over his eyes, taking care not to bump the tender bridge of his nose. *Damn. I wish I could have said goodbye to the princess—especially since it would probably be the last thing I ever did say to her.*

Allysian is so damnably independent. And the bravest girl I ever met. I could serve such a queen with pride.

Although I rather doubt I'll get that chance. Fathers in general tend to be angered by young men who compromise their daughters' virtue—whether imagined or not—and a king holds the power to act on such perceived indiscretions.

Digan well knew the king's temper.

No matter whose fault it might actually be that Allysian followed me, the king will punish the only person he can possibly blame...and, as I did when we were children, I will gladly shoulder that blame.

Digan groaned.

I am becoming increasingly maudlin as the night wears on.

There was a surreptitious noise outside the doorway, and Digan looked up. "What are you doing here?" he scolded, keeping his voice soft with difficulty.

He rose stiffly to his feet and crossing to the barred opening. "You silly little fool! By the goddess, Allysian! Don't you know that this will help neither of us? Your father is already looking to stretch my neck. Do you want to give him further cause?"

Allysian gulped, her face paling at the vehemence of his words. She pulled her hand from behind her back. Shyly, she held out her well-worn practice lute. "I brought you a present...I know it's not the one you wanted—"

Her face twisted, and she leaned the instrument against the bars, reaching a hand through to take his. "Oh, Digan...I had to see you. Gauston told me they brought you here."

"Gauston?"

"He came to tell me that the watch arrested you. He is watching the door."

All his bravado fled away, and he let his heart speak for him. "I can't believe you're here. It's like a dream," he murmured, lifting a hand to her cheek.

"Oh, Digan! Papa is so furious with me, but I

needed to make sure that you were all right. I don't understand why they put you here. I told Papa you were responsible for making sure that I got home safely, but he just wouldn't listen..."

"It isn't your fault, Sian. You did your best."

Allysian's eyes shone with unshed tears. "I am such a fool, Digan. I didn't know any of this would happen. I just didn't think! You probably feel that I am a hopeless idiot."

Mordigan stared down at the girl with a fond smile. "No, dearest...I think you are the most beautiful, headstrong, impossible girl I ever met. I have never known anyone as gentle or courageous." He let his hand trail down the side of her face. "And whether you believe me or not...I cannot lie."

She looked up at him, the tears threatening to overflow. "You have changed so much, Mordigan Bryre. Even though I fancied I loved you, I knew you weren't perfect. But the vain self-important liar I thought I knew before would never have gone to such lengths for me as you have done. You have risked so much—"

"I was the fool. Allysian, I may never get another chance to say this to you..." His voice caught in his throat when he realized how true the statement was. "I think you are the most wonderful woman I know, and I love you with all my heart and soul. Whatever I may say before the king tomorrow... always remember that I love you. Nothing will ever change that."

"Why are you telling me this now?" She caught his hand. "What are you *not* telling me?"

"I-I can't tell you anything more, Allysian. Please don't ask me to." He pulled away from her and picked up her lute from the floor outside the cell. It would not fit through the bars, but it was comforting in his hands. He strummed the strings absently.

"Digan, please—why can't you trust me?"

"Allysian, I would give my soul to tell you everything...but I can't! Not today. Perhaps not ever. But it's not because I don't trust you. I made a promise—"

"—To a lady," she finished, her voice bitter as she turned away from him.

Digan turned to his music in an instinctive search for comfort. He began to play the tune he was working on the miserable day this whole catastrophe started...the day of his disgrace...the day she first came after him with her hair flying out behind her like a sunlit cloud...his father's song?

But today, he sang a new verse. His own verse. His pure tenor echoed sweetly in the stone chamber.

The time we've spent together
has been my greatest treasure...
And though I now must
leave you, I will love you
till I die...

He faltered to a halt, unable to go on. The words were too real. Setting the instrument on the ground outside the bars, he sank to the floor, resting forehead on bent knees. The thought of what he would be sacrificing overwhelmed him, though he never for a moment contemplated another choice.

It is a small enough price to pay to save Allysian from her own folly.

The princess knelt on the floor outside the cell, both hands gripping the bars hard. "What is it, Digan? Please—tell me!"

I know that if I tell her the truth, she will only try to dissuade me...

And so—he lied. "I was thinking of my father." He could feel the pain in his throat, and his voice broke. He cleared it with a rough cough. "I wonder what he would think of me." That much was true, and his voice strengthened accordingly.

"I think he would be very proud of you, Mordigan Bryre," she answered in a soft whisper. "I know I am."

"I hope you're right..." He looked up at her, and smiled regretfully. "I never knew him. Or my mother. They died before I was old enough to remember..."

"Digan—"

"Yes?"

Allysian stretched both arms through the bars. "Please..." She was wearing a beautiful silken gown, which flowed over the stones of the corridor in a shimmering blue-green sea.

By the goddess, she is so beautiful.

He turned to face her, kneeling on his side of the bars. "Sian, I—"

"Shh...don't talk." She put a finger to his lips. "We haven't much time. Papa will be missing me soon."

"But there's so very much I want to say to you—"

"There will be plenty of time for talking later..."

He let it go for now. *There is no point in arguing with her and wasting what little precious time we have to spend together. She will learn the truth soon enough.*

With a heavy sigh, he took her hands where they

rested on the bars and rested his forehead on the cold iron.

Allysian pulled one of her hands free, and raised his chin. "I thought *I* was supposed to be the shy, demure one," she murmured with a half-smile. "Would you please kiss me?"

He returned her smile. "Is that a command, Your Highness?"

"Oh, most definitely," she replied, breathlessly.

He obeyed the order.

"Lady—" Gauston's soft call from the head of the stairs came much too soon. "We must go back. It's getting late."

Allysian broke away from Digan with a regretful sigh. "I must leave, my dearest. Papa may come looking for me. Dame Madeline locked me in my room for the night..."

"Oh, Allysian—what have I done to you?"

"It's not your fault, Digan. I brought it on myself." She brushed the hair out of his eyes with a gentle hand, that crow-wing silk fringe that absolutely refused to behave itself. "But I'm glad that I went after you. I'd do it all again in a minute."

He got to his feet, raising her up and favoring her with his crooked smile. "So, you liked being chained to the wall? Is there anything else you want to tell me?"

She felt her cheeks crimson at his jest. "Oh, Digan...I do love you so." She hugged him through the bars, laying her head against the cold iron.

He dropped a kiss on the top of her hair. "Go along with you now, before they come looking for you. You mustn't be found here."

She started down the hallway, turning and looking back over her shoulder.

Mordigan stood with bowed head, guard dropped for the moment, looking so intolerably alone that she almost returned to the cell.

Just then, Digan glanced up and caught her eye upon him. He gave her an exaggerated frown and shooed her along with a gesture.

Her hand was on the door to the corridor when she heard a low call behind her. "I love you too, my dearest princess."

She lost her tight rein on her courage, and fled the dungeon, not daring to look back. Gauston was right behind her. When they made it safely past the sleeping sentry to a deserted corridor, Allysian crumpled to the stone floor and let the tears come, sobbing bitterly.

The boy hunkered down beside her and laid a timid hand on her shoulder. "Don't cry, my lady. All will be well—"

"How can it be, Gauston? My father—my father will hang Digan if he can, and it is all my fault!"

"There must be *someone* who can help..."

Allysian stared at the boy with a sudden wild hope. "Of course! I must get word to—" She scrambled to her feet, grabbing Gauston's hand and dragging him along after her. "You are going to do me one more favor, my boy. I need you to take a message to someone for me as quickly as you possibly can. But first, you must lock me in my chamber."

She gave the boy no chance to argue, plans fomenting as they sped through the hallways. *All will be well. I won't allow it to be any other way.*

Far too early the next morning, Mordigan Bryre stood once again before a court of law, chin lifted at a proud angle...but this time, he held absolutely no doubt of the judgment. Meeting the steel-eyed glare of the king with a level gaze, he waited for the inescapable outcome.

"Speak up, boy. This is your chance to present your case. Have you any defense to offer for your actions?" asked Vasileios.

"No, my lord," Digan murmured, stealing a glance at Allysian, who hovered behind her father's throne, white-faced with anxiety.

"Did you know that the princess would come after you?"

It was the first step toward the scaffold, but Digan took it willingly. "I suspected she might." He allowed a trace of his former arrogance to slip into his voice, and his pose shifted almost imperceptibly to become that of a handsome man confident in his attraction for the weaker sex. "I knew that she was interested in me, and I guessed she might be amenable to the suggestion." His voice rasped at the lie, and he coughed against the spasm of pain in his throat.

Please, Lady Hathor...let me see her safely out of this mess before my voice fades completely. If I can take the full blame, she can get on with her life, and there will be no more locked doors in the night.

The king's face was becoming an alarming shade of purple, but his words were delivered with an icy calm. "And what gave you reason to deduce this interest?"

Digan favored Vasileios with an oily smirk. "The way she stared at me during her lute lessons, the sighs she gave whenever she saw me walk by—" He was forced to clear his throat several times before he could continue. "It was obvious that she was attracted to me."

He caught sight of Cormeyer standing in the front rank of the assembled courtiers, and swallowed hard at the disgust on his former master's expressive features. "It amused me to lead her on...to see how far she was willing to go." His voice was sandpaper rough in a throat that burned like fire.

Allysian's brows were drawn together in a puzzled frown, and Digan's heart sank. *I am altogether too accomplished a liar...she is beginning to doubt me herself.*

Perhaps that is for the best. Better that she be angry and hurt for a time than mourn me. It will be easier for her to move forward if she isn't looking back.

He crossed his arms across his breast with a casual insolence, and gave the girl a broad, suggestive wink.

Allysian flushed and turned away.

Digan hugged himself surreptitiously to stop his trembling. *I've never felt so completely alone in my life.*

The king grated out, "Are you saying that you harbored illicit designs on my daughter?"

Digan yawned, covering his mouth with a negligent hand only when the gesture had gone past being polite to merely compounding the rudeness. "Heavens no, my lord—I didn't really think that much about the girl one way or the other."

The statement was true enough to earn him a moment's respite from the pain, and he swallowed gratefully. *Whenever I did think of her, I always considered the princess far above me. I never even dreamed that she noticed me as anything more than a childhood playmate.*

Allysian fled from the dais, and Mordigan felt his heart lurch in his chest. How he longed to tell her the truth, to comfort her, but there was nothing more to say. *If she no longer believes the vows I made to her last night, then at least there is a chance she will find happiness in time. It will not be my problem to worry about much longer.*

Vasileios held something up in his hand. It took Digan a puzzled moment to make out the golden comb that Allysian gave him that day on the road—the one that Payter stole from his belt pouch. Digan bit his lip.

"Do you recognize this?" asked the king.

"Should I?"

"It was in his belt pouch! I can bear witness, my lord king!" Payter shoved his way to the front of the crowd, chest puffed out with self-importance as he pointed at Digan with a triumphant cry. "He must have stolen it from Her Highness without her knowledge."

"How do you answer this further charge, Mordigan Bryre?"

Thank the goddess Allysian is not present to contradict me.

"The girl may have given it to me...I really don't remember. So many girls give me so many things." He could barely choke out the final words of the sentence, and only a paroxysm of coughing cleared his throat enough to go on. "'Tis the curse of a handsome face."

"You led my daughter astray merely to toy with her! You have no feelings for her?" Vasileios shouted, face livid with anger.

Mordigan took a deep breath—*this is the moment. This will be the greatest lie of my life, and it will seal my fate beyond redemption.*

Lifting his chin once more, he drawled negligently, "None whatsoever, Your Majesty."

A knifing pain drove Digan to his knees, his hand reflexively encircling his throat as wave upon wave of volcanic fire roared through it. He could not even gasp aloud. No sound escaped his lips, though his soul screamed in anguish.

"Do you have anything further to say?" asked the king.

Unable to reply, Mordigan shook his head in numb denial.

"Then hear my decree." Vasileios erupted to his feet and pointed a quivering finger at the kneeling youth. "Mordigan Bryre, you have proven yourself to be a liar, and a thief. Moreover, you willfully and cold-heartedly compromised the Princess Allysian's honor and led her to run away with you in an attempt to further your lascivious designs.

"She was foolish to allow it, but she is a mere child of fifteen. You, on the other hand, are now a responsible adult, and must be held accountable for your actions. It was criminal of you to encourage her. This can be viewed as an act of deliberate treason, for the stain of this matter will never be removed. Her reputation has been irreparably damaged.

"There is only one fitting punishment for treason.

Tomorrow at dawn, you shall be hung by the neck until dead."

Mordigan slumped further where he knelt, nodding his head in silent acceptance of his sentence. *I expected no other.*

"Have you any last defense?" asked the king. "If so, speak now. This is your final audience."

Digan shook his head.

There is nothing more for me to say, even if I could voice the words. To admit that, in truth, I love the girl with all my heart will not endear me to the king, and it is likely to cause Allysian more trouble in the end.

"Take him back to his cell," ordered Vasileios, gesturing toward the prisoner as he turned away.

Mordigan allowed himself to be lifted to his feet, and stumbled out of the audience chamber, supported between two of the palace guard. One of the guards was Garad, his face white as a sheet, mouth drawn with pity.

Digan hung his head.

As they entered the hallway, his heart twisted painfully as he glimpsed Allysian half-concealed behind a pillar. Against his better judgment, Digan mouthed the word "Remember..." his soul crying out through his emerald eyes.

Allysian flushed and looked away.

Digan gulped and the guards dragged him on down the hallway. For the first—and last—time in his life, Digan looked back. Head turned over his shoulder; he kept the girl in sight as long as he possibly could, impressing her image upon his heart.

It was too much to bear, that indifferent drawl as

Digan said such horrible things about her. Allysian didn't know what to believe anymore. One minute, Digan swore that he loved her with all his soul, and the next, he made her affection seem like a mere trifle which he considered a handsome lad's due reward. She couldn't listen to any more of the trial, and fled the court, fighting the tears.

In the corridor outside the throne room, she hid behind a pillar and took deep, shuddering breaths to combat the rising sobs.

I will not weep for him again. I will not!

"Tut, tut, little princess—do not give up on the lad so easily. Is this why you battled so hard to save him? To see him hang by your father's hand? I thought better of you."

The creaking voice was no surprise. "Did I not send Gauston to find the witch?"

But Allysian surprised them both by throwing herself into Freitanya's arms with a sob. "How can I save him now? Oh, my lady—"

The witch patted her on the shoulder with an awkward hand. "All will be well, little one. Do not fret. I must speak with someone who owes us both—your Mordigan and me—and then I will come to you. Expect me before morning, and the plan will be laid." The wizened crone bent forward and gently kissed the smooth cheek damp with tears.

"Love is a precious thing, princess. Such a deep vein of it cannot be tossed aside so easily. Your Mordigan Bryre is far too special to hang. Trust me."

Allysian gazed up at the witch. "Please, my lady. Save him. I will do anything you ask."

The witch smiled, and the expression transformed her withered face into something beautiful. "Don't worry. We will save him together, my sweet. You and I...and the one who owes him most."

Before Allysian could question Freitanya further on this mysterious statement, the witch vanished, and the door to the throne room was flung open. The princess ducked further behind the pillar, swiping the tears from her face. She saw them lead Digan out, and caught the message that he sent her. "Remember..."

She turned away, unable to face him, to betray the hope that warred with confusion in her breast. *Remember? How could I ever forget?*

Late that night, Allysian came to him, as he feared she would. She stood before the barred door and studied him, her blue eyes grave. Digan stood before her, meeting her gaze squarely. He could see the marks of tears on her face, and her eyes were red and swollen.

I hate myself for causing her such pain, but I don't know how to ease it.

"You were lying." The flat tone made it a statement, not a question.

Unable to reply, Digan nodded.

Her hand flashed through the bars to strike his cheek.

The blow caught him off guard, and his head rocked from the slap. It was hard enough to split his lip, and he licked away blood at the corner of his mouth, his nose throbbing violently.

"How dare you!" she hissed.

Digan was confused for a moment. And then, all at once, he understood. *She believes the lie was spoken last night, when I told her that I loved her. She really thinks I was toying with her the whole time. Allysian believes my lies to Vasileios. She thinks...*

He gripped the bars between them and let his head rest against the cold iron. Despair washed over him in crashing waves that left him breathless.

Damnation.

Digan felt a tentative touch on his shoulder, and he looked up, eyes filled with unashamed tears.

"You lied today," she whispered. "Before the court?"

He nodded miserably.

Allysian's face lit up. "Then you *did* mean what you said last night?"

Digan reached a trembling hand through the bars and touched her cheek. He nodded again.

"She said you did, but I've been so confused...I should have known." She cradled his hand in hers, and kissed it. "What are you going to do?"

"Nothing," he mouthed.

"Nothing! But Digan—"

He shook his head and pulled away, crossing to sink down on the edge of his stone cot. "Nothing," he repeated soundlessly.

"You can't simply give up. You can't be prepared to die like this, Digan! You can't!"

He shrugged.

"Mordigan Bryre...speak to me, damn you!" The color was high in her cheeks, and her eyes glittered with angry tears.

It was obvious that she was at the end of her strength, and he ached to comfort her with the pretty words that once came so easily to him.

"I can't," he mouthed, pointing to his throat and shaking his head.

"What's wrong with you?" Allysian cried, stamping her foot in fury. "Why won't you talk to me!"

"I can't," he repeated silently, taking great pains to make each word distinct. "I can't speak."

"You certainly could earlier!" she shouted, beginning to pace before the cell. It appeared almost as if *she* were the one caged, and he the watcher. "I don't know what to believe anymore! You said last night that you loved me, and today..." Her voice broke.

Visibly collecting herself, she continued. "Today you swear before the king that you never cared for me at all. And even now you won't speak in your own defense. Perhaps that is because my father was right all along—you are a traitorous scoundrel who...who wanted merely to take advantage of me."

Her words cut him like daggers, and he sank further and further into himself on the hard stone bunk, finally burying face in hands. It hurt so grievously to hear her angry accusations. She was talking herself into believing the lie after all.

"Digan." Allysian's call was soft, and the anger was gone.

He raised eyes awash with tears to find that she was kneeling on the stone of the corridor, her arms once more stretched toward him through the bars.

Mordigan rose to unsteady feet and dropped to his

own knees on his side of the bars. He hugged her fiercely through the narrow grill, longing for the freedom that always seemed such a given thing, and not a precious treasure. If only I could tell her everything!

"I don't want to lose you," Allysian moaned, clinging to him just as tightly. "If you won't do anything, then I shall!"

Digan didn't bother trying to answer. He merely held the slim princess in his arms as she wept, his own tears sliding openly down his ashen face. They were both emotionally exhausted.

To have come so far together and have it end like this... but what could she possibly hope to do to prevent it?

Digan allowed himself a moment to dream—she would find a way, and they would be free to be together—but reality soon raced an unwelcome head.

No, the morning will come—and far too quickly. The king will have his scapegoat. For now, I will comfort as I can.

Finally, Allysian cried herself to sleep, cheek pressed against the cold bars that separated them.

Digan remained sitting on the hard stone floor, cradling her clumsily through the grill. He studied her sleeping features with wonder.

She is a princess, and she cares for a nobody like me...

He brushed the golden hair from her brow with a tender hand, and kissed her forehead awkwardly.

"You risk much, young Bryre," came an amused voice from the corridor.

Digan's head snapped up in panic, and his arm tightened instinctively around Allysian. Somehow, he was not altogether surprised to see Freitanya standing before him.

After all, she began this whole affair.

His shoulders sagged.

"So, you could not do it, could you?" continued the witch, voice filled with laughter. "You could not resist lying and speak only the truth—not even to save your own life." She cackled aloud at that, and Allysian stirred in her sleep.

Digan raised finger to lips, eyes pleading eloquently for the witch's silence.

Freitanya made a pass of her own hand, muttering under her breath. Allysian sighed, shifting in her sleep.

Digan tensed.

"Don't worry, young lover," the witch teased. "I have not harmed your beloved. Merely insured that she will not wake and interrupt us. What chance has a poor withered crone like me to keep your attention if a flower such as she vies for it? What, none of your pretty words now? Stand up, boy. I'm getting a crick in my neck peering down at you."

Digan eased Allysian to the floor, and rose to his feet. He met the witch's eye bravely.

Freitanya tittered at his set expression. "I won't bite you, boy! Actually, I am very proud of you, Mordigan Bryre. You have made quite a noble sacrifice for your lady love. Does she truly appreciate its gravity, I wonder?"

Digan bit his lip; thumb straying unbidden to the split corner of his mouth.

"I see she does not," bubbled the witch in amusement. "Truly a feisty wench. A worthy match for a boy like you."

His mouth curled in a rueful, self-mocking smile.

The witch's face softened. "My poor boy...you have no idea how special you really are."

Digan shrugged and started to turn away.

"I give you one wish, Mordigan Bryre. You may speak that wish despite the curse—I am no lip reader—and whatever one thing you wish for *will* be granted."

Digan cleared his throat, swallowed heavily, and then croaked out in a hoarse whisper, "Take care of her for me."

He could see that his wish took the witch by surprise.

"You will not reconsider...wish yourself to the Seven Kingdoms, or erase Vasileios' wrath? You really love the girl that much? To waste such a gift on another when your own circumstances are so desperate?"

Digan nodded. "I do," he mouthed, mute once more.

"It shall be done," Freitanya replied solemnly, her dark eyes somber. "Sleep now, boy. You need the rest." She waved her hand, and Digan slumped to the floor, lids heavy despite his best efforts to stay awake. His eyes closed to hooded slits.

"Poor, brave child," she whispered, shaking her head. "You have been ill-used. But soon the full truth shall be seen."

Digan watched, with dazed eyes as the withered crone raised her arms over her head and recited the words of a spell.

A shuddering ripple ran over her, and she was transformed. When the spell was complete, all that remained of the hag Freitanya was her long, white hair. The body of the newly altered witch was the voluptuous form of the woodcutter's wife, and the sweet face was that of the young wolf-girl Digan met in the forest clearing.

He struggled to awaken, disbelieving what he had seen, but his eyes drifted shut. As consciousness faded, he heard the witch murmur, "Rest easy, Mordigan Bryre. Those who love you will see you live, and you will come into your own at last!"

With a final wave of her arms, she was gone, and Digan slept.

CHAPTER 10

IT WAS A WARM spring day, and he perched in one of the trees lining the park outside the Hall. He was playing on a golden lute, the notes rivaling birdsong. Glancing down through the net of greenery, he saw Allysian wandering along the path, her nose buried in one of her books. He grinned to himself, carefully laying the lute across the crook of branches beside him, and swung down in front of the princess.

"Oh!"

He laughed at the surprise on her face. "Whither do you wander, lady?"

She smiled at him, holding out her hand. "Wherever you wish, my lord."

He reached to take her outstretched hand...

...and the dream vanished. Digan found himself alone. The cold of the stone floor seeped through his worn finery, permeating his very bones. He rose to his feet with a stifled sigh, rubbing a stiff neck as he went to stand beneath the high window.

The gray tinge to the sky warned that dawn was fast approaching, and he forced himself to breathe. *It is time. Oh, Lady Hathor...*

But for once his prayers failed him. He could think of nothing to say.

At the sound of ringing footsteps advancing down the corridor, Digan whirled. He ran his hands through his disheveled black waves to smooth his hair, and tugged his tattered garments into place, gulping down a rush of panic.

I will not let them see the terror. I must be strong. It is all I have.

He turned to face the door, standing proud and straight as they came for him.

One of the guards unlocked the bars with a heavy iron key, and another strode into the cell, manacles in hand. It was Garad, eyes full of sympathy.

Mordigan blanched. Somehow, having the cadet chain him made the ordeal worse, but he held his wrists out before him, relieved to see that his hands were steady.

"Those won't be necessary," stated a clipped voice from behind the soldiers.

Digan started, and fell to one knee instinctively, head bowed.

Vasileios stepped forward and laid a hand on the boy's shoulder. "Arise, Mordigan Bryre."

Dazed by the gentleness of the king's tone, Digan obeyed. His mind whirled with questions, but he knew no way to express them...so he did not try, waiting patiently to see what the king's visit portended.

"I was allowed little sleep this night," the king began. "Allysian never knew her mother. Perhaps it is in an attempt to compensate for that lack that she has been so woefully spoiled. It is rare that she finds herself denied any whim. She came to me and begged that I speak to you once more—that I give you one final chance to explain what really occurred. She claims full responsibility for her own actions, and says that you had no idea that she followed you until you rescued her from a Nausaen dungeon despite the dangers to yourself. Is this true?"

Digan shook his head with stubborn determination.

I am not going to let her take the blame. There is no need to drag her down with me. My own life is already forfeit. I refuse to ruin hers.

The king eyed him coolly. "Are you calling my daughter a liar?"

Mobile mouth twisting at the irony of it, Digan gave an emphatic nod.

"And you have no explanation as to why she might do such a thing?"

The youth shrugged.

"Have you *anything* to say for yourself at all?"

With a heavy sigh, Digan shook his head once more.

"Very well," murmured the king. "I have no choice but to carry out the sentence as decreed. For what it is worth, my boy—I am sorry. You are hiding something, and I believe I can guess what that might be. It does you credit. I wish circumstances were different...and I will miss your songs."

Vasileios nodded to the guards standing at attention, and Garad stepped forward to take Mordigan's arm.

Digan inhaled deeply, and then released the breath with a shaky sigh, throwing back his shoulders. He staggered a step as he started toward the door—his legs a trifle unwilling to obey him—but he forced himself to keep moving, determined to keep his dignity at least.

The journey through the castle was a painful

reminder of happier days. Though the corridors surrounding the dungeon were unfamiliar to him, as they ascended, the hallways were filled with memories.

There is where Allysian tripped and sprained her ankle. I carried her back to the tower so Dame Madeline wouldn't find out she was running where she was forbidden to play.

That is where I sang for Vasileios and the envoy from Suranaka. It was my best performance ever.

Oh, by the goddess...what have I done? Is it worth it?

Allysian's earnest little face flashed across his thoughts.

Yes. In the end, it is.

The passage through the castle seemed interminable, but they emerged at last in a small courtyard. It was deserted, and Digan allowed himself a sigh of relief.

At least it will be a private execution...

But the guards continued forward, sweeping him along before them like a leaf in a stream. A gate was thrown open, and Mordigan's heart plummeted in his chest with a physical jolt of pain.

The square outside was filled with spectators. Some were drawn to the sight simply for the spectacle, but Digan recognized all too many of the faces. The shop boys and other apprentices were huddled in small groups throughout the crowd; Roelf and Tolin standing together in a doorway; Sult with his arm around Garad's Matilde as if to offer comfort. Payter grinned like a hungry wolf from a perch atop a lamppost. There were shopkeepers Digan once insulted, street vendors he pilfered sweetmeats from, and in a sheltered corner the tall figure of Cormeyer, lips pressed tightly together.

Digan's vision blurred, and he blinked to clear it. Nowhere did he catch the eye of anyone who showed the least regret for what was to come...and the one face he both longed and dreaded to see was conspicuously absent.

Garad's hand was a welcome support as Mordigan hung his head.

Perhaps that absence is for the best. I really don't think I would have the courage to be brave if she was watching, and I must be. I have no other legacy to leave—I must die with dignity.

Digan tossed his dark hair out of his eyes and stepped out of the courtyard gate. The air filled with an instantaneous hornet-buzz of whispered conversations. He caught a blur of movement out of the corner of his eye, and blinked.

Is that Jedrek? And Sayre?

He heard Payter's frenzied shout of "It's no more than you deserve, Mordigan Bryre!" and was ashamed to think that the other boy was quite probably right.

Even though I am innocent of spiriting away the princess, I committed plenty of other wickedness in my time. In a fit of temper, I always strike first and think later; my lies hurt friend and foe alike; and my petty thievery was more from boredom than need. Maybe I will be better off dead. At least I will no longer disappoint those who care for me.

Lost in thought, Mordigan reached the bottom of the scaffold without realizing it. Confronted suddenly with a wooden stairway, he glanced up, a puzzled frown etched between his brows.

He caught sight of the rope dangling above him and suddenly swayed forward, all the strength gone from his legs. Digan half-fell against the balustrade before he could catch himself, and he heard the whispers intensify around him.

Feeling a steadying hand at his elbow, he glanced down to find Gauston beside him. He gave the boy a grateful smile.

The little thief gave him an encouraging nod in return. "All will be well," the boy whispered.

Digan choked back the bitter laugh that rose in his throat.

I suppose it will at that.

Steeling himself to continue, he mounted the staircase and climbed to the platform unassisted. He stood statue-still beneath the noose, uncertain what to do next. Forcing himself to breathe evenly, he hid his shaking hands against his sides.

I wish that the king insisted on the manacles after all. I fear I shall disgrace myself further by clawing at the noose as it tightens. Oh, Great Hathor...

Mordigan gulped, a wave of dizziness swirling through him. *I am lost—utterly, utterly lost.*

The Lord High Executioner loomed beside his lever. As Digan fought to remain upright on his feet, the hangman stepped forward. Behind his traditional black hood, the executioner's gray eyes were kind, and Digan felt a measure of calm restore his balance.

In a strangely familiar voice, the hangman murmured, "Take heart, my boy. What must be done will be—what will be done must be."

The words were also familiar, and Digan almost missed the next question as he tried to remember where he first heard them.

"Would it comfort you to bind your hands?" continued the executioner, his tone gentle.

Startled by the sound of his own thoughts put into words, Digan nodded gratefully.

With the deft twist of a silken cord, the man secured the boy's hands behind his back.

"Is there anything else you wish?" asked the hangman.

Digan shook his head, staring down at the rough wooden floor of the platform so that he didn't have to see the rope swinging above him. *I just want it to be over.*

"Kneel down," the executioner prompted, and Digan fell to one knee, clumsy without the use of his hands for balance. "Receive the Prayer of Absolution."

A slim figure stepped forward from the shadowy corner of the platform, features hidden by a deep cowl. Digan glanced up, and caught his breath with a silent hiss.

Allysian raised one hand in a gesture of benediction.

Digan stared at her hungrily; now doubly glad for the silk cord that stopped his hands from reaching for her.

She spoke the words to the simple prayer of forgiveness. "In life, there are many roads to travel. Sometimes the wisest feet stray from the path. Hathor forgives the penitent, and welcomes them to Her rest.

Do you repent the wickedness you have done?"

He nodded.

"Accept then the forgiveness of the Divine Lady. Peace be with you, my son," she finished and then bent to deliver the requisite kiss upon his brow. "I love you, Mordigan Bryre," she whispered, her breath stirring his hair.

He tilted his face toward her and mouthed, "I love you..."

Eyes sparkling with tears, she nodded to the executioner, and the hangman helped Digan to his feet. Conscious only of the princess, and that he must spare her what he could, Digan stood quietly waiting.

The king mounted the platform now, and Allysian pulled her hood further forward.

Digan could no longer see her beloved features, but they were engraved on his heart.

Vasileios gestured to the Lord High Executioner, and the hangman stepped forward once more to fit the rope about Digan's neck. His throat tightened in an involuntary spasm at the touch of the rough hemp as the noose was drawn over his head, and he gave a ragged cough.

By the goddess...it is really happening. I am going to die.

Allysian turned away, and Digan closed his eyes. Only the pull of the rope kept him on his feet.

"Be ready for anything, my son," murmured the executioner.

Before there was time for Digan to consider what the hangman meant, a commotion broke out in the crowd beneath the scaffold. He thought he heard

Jedrek bellow, and somewhere a woman's scream. A howl arose that sounded suspiciously like Payter.

There was a confusion of shouted orders from the king and the guards scattered throughout the spectators. Digan's eyes flew open in time to see the hangman pull his lever, and then the floor dropped from beneath his feet, and he was falling.

Digan fought the panic shrieking in his breast for release. The rope tightened in an inexorable grip about his throat, choking the life out of him, and the fall seemed to last for hours.

Allysian!

His soul screamed what he could not. And then a black and red darkness engulfed him.

Allysian saw Digan's stumble at the foot of the gallows, and her heart went out to him. *He looks so lost and vulnerable.*

She longed with every fiber of her soul to reach out and cradle him in her arms...to reassure him that all would be well...but she must play her own part if the future was to be salvaged.

Despite, or perhaps because of, her father's overindulgences, Allysian developed her fiercely independent spirit.

If Digan will not help himself, then I will do it for him—just as I got him into this mess in the first place by running off after him.

She was no longer angry with her father, knowing that his own law tied his hands in the matter. Since Digan even now stood upon the gallows' platform, he did not recant his confession. Somehow, she never expected him to, and so slipped into her habit to fill her part in Freitanya's plot.

While Digan dreamed his peaceful woodland dreams the night before, Allysian sat in huddled consultation with the witch.

"Why will he not talk to me?" she sobbed, held in the witch's comforting embrace.

"He can't, child," Freitanya soothed.

"What do you mean?"

"He has given up his voice for you. It was a freely made choice."

"What are you saying?"

"He was under enchantment, Allysian—to lie cost him the thing he held most dear. He did it to protect your honor, lovey. He would not let you take the blame, and so he lied to your father and said that you meant nothing to him. It was the greatest lie he could possibly tell, and he did it knowing that he would be giving up his speech forever. That is truly love, Allysian. Hold it dear."

The enchantress revealed other secrets to the princess, all shedding more light on Digan's evasions and silences.

"I didn't think it was possible, but now I love him even more. Oh, my lady, what must I do?"

On the witch's advice, Allysian persuaded her father to talk to Digan one last time because she knew that Vasileios would expect her to do so. However, her true faith rested in the witch—and in the unexpected ally that Freitanya brought to the council.

For her own part, Allysian found a sleepy stable boy who knew where to find Gauston in the dead of night, and she brought the little thief into their circle...

Allysian returned to the present with a jolt, taking a deep breath as the executioner motioned her forward to stand before Digan. She crossed her fingers that everything was in place. She recited the prayer Freitanya taught her the night before, and then whispered, "I love you, Mordigan Bryre."

I wish I could tell him more...that I understand it all now...that I am touched to the core by the sacrifice he made for my honor...that I would give him my life if he asked for it.

She saw him mouth his response, and knowing the truth behind his silence almost undid her resolve. As her father moved into his place, Allysian drew her cowl more securely into place, and nodded to the executioner.

He moved forward to help Digan to his feet. Under cover of his movement, Allysian leaned over the railing of the platform, and gave Gauston the surreptitious signal he waited for at the foot of the stairs.

The boy sprinted off into the crowd, one hand reaching for his sling even as he moved. There was a bellow of rage from a male voice as Gauston nodded to one of his friends in the crowd. Simultaneously, on the far side of the square, a querulous female voice was raised in enraged outcry. From this distance, it was impossible to make out the words, but the tone was one of righteous indignation. Before the resulting hubbub died away, there was a single startled howl from nearer at hand, telling her Gauston's stone found its mark.

Serves that wretched Payter Fletcher right, too! Allysian thought with satisfaction.

As the multiple incidents in the crowd drew attention elsewhere, the guardsmen in the square were distracted away from the scaffold.

When Vasileios gestured to the executioner to

pull the lever, Allysian took a deep breath. *This is the critical moment.*

She reached out and took her father's arm, laying her other hand over the executioner's as he released the trap beneath Digan's feet.

By the Seven, Hathor, and all the hands of Fate, let this work! Allysian closed her eyes as a shiver seemed to run through the platform. There was a clap of thunder, and her lungs were suddenly filled with a mixture of wood smoke and the exquisite scent of roses.

She held a lungful of the perfumed air and let her lids flutter open. Instantly, she dropped her hold on her father's arm and fell to her knees beside Digan's motionless form in the midst of the flower-strewn field. She lifted the boy's head into her lap, and removed the noose, leaving an ugly bruising around his throat.

"Let me take him, my dear," came the melodious voice of the "Lord High Executioner," who now threw aside his hood. The man lifted the unconscious Digan into his arms as if the tall apprentice were a mere babe. "See to your father, Allysian. I believe His Majesty is looking a bit dazed." With a nod at Vasileios, who did indeed look rather lost, the executioner turned to lead the way toward a distant tower shimmering in the sun.

Allysian took her father by the hand, and flashed him a tentative smile. "I do love him so, Papa...I couldn't just let you hang him for a crime that wasn't his fault. I had to do something."

With a rueful smile of his own, Vasileios shook his head at his daughter. "I think perhaps you better begin at the beginning, my dearest girl. I have a feeling that I came into the middle of something... miraculous."

Their guide turned and called back to the king. "Do not worry, my lord. It will all be explained. But we must wait for our other conspirators to arrive... and, more-to-the-point, the revels cannot begin without our star player.

"Mordigan will rejoin us soon, and all will be revealed. Until then, I must put the boy to bed. He is not as light as he looks."

With a little giggle of happiness, Allysian threaded her arm through that of Vasileios, and led him after their host.

An unknown eternity later, Digan felt himself rising up out of the darkness like an air bubble in a cup of beer. It was an odd sensation.

Am I dead? he wondered absently. *It seems a reasonable assumption. Most men who are hung by the neck do, in fact, die. But, if I am dead, why does my throat ache so damnably much?*

Perhaps I am in hell.

Digan did not doubt in the least that he deserved such an ending. He wasn't entirely sure that he wanted to know the truth if that were the case, however, so he kept his eyes squeezed shut.

"Why doesn't he wake up?" complained a familiar voice, and Digan's heart leapt up—then crashed in his chest—leaving his head swimming.

Why is she *here if this is hell? Or did I ruin her after all? Drag her down with me? No...*he moaned silently, *Freitanya* promised *me...*

"I believe he does but counterfeit, my dear," came

an amused answer. The voice was that of the Lord High Executioner, but with his eyes closed, Digan knew where he had heard that voice before—and he was even less sure that he wanted to open his eyes.

"Come, come, boy!" continued the voice. "Reassure your lady fair."

When it was put to him in those terms, there was no choice but to obey. Reluctantly, he lifted his lids, focusing a bleary glance on the group of faces bent over him. He blinked, and they sharpened—Allysian, Vasileios, Freitanya, a grinning Gauston...and Talthos.

It was the wizard that most confused Digan. Their parting was hardly amicable—and yet Talthos' hand must have been behind this rescue—if such it was.

"Do not try to reason it out," laughed Freitanya. "All will be told in time." She eased an arm beneath Digan's shoulders and helped him to sit up. The witch exhibited surprising strength for a woman of her age and build. "How is your throat?"

It feels as if a giant hand lifted me and squeezed it like a grape, he thought, but merely shrugged. *Complaining will not ease it, and I am grateful simply to be alive.*

"As you see, boy," the witch cackled, placing an arm around Allysian's slim waist, "I kept my promise. But the only way I could take care of the girl as you asked was to save your worthless hide, so your noble sacrifice was partly in vain."

The witch eyed him with obvious affection. "What shall we do with you, Mordigan Bryre? A hero despite yourself...that's what you are."

"I'm no hero—" protested Digan, and then stopped in surprise as he realized that the words were spoken aloud.

Admittedly, my voice is hoarse and broken, but I definitely spoke *those words.*

"Your voice will never be the same," Talthos warned, "but some sacrifices are *too* noble. I would not have you lose everything you hold dear when you acted as you did merely to keep your promises to us." He moved to the far side of the room, and lifted an object from a chair. "I too have something for you, my boy."

Talthos placed the long-promised lute into Digan's hands, smiling at the expression of bewildered wonder that the gift inspired.

Digan brushed the strings with one hand. The sound of the magical instrument was like molten gold, pure as crystal, and sweet as honey. It lifted his heart merely to hear the dulcet chords.

"As I said, the magic involved in such an instrument is very powerful and costly—did you think I would waste my efforts so easily? And yours? You will still have your music, lad." The wizard sighed. "I'm afraid, however, that you will never have the voice to sing again...and it is a pity, for you inherited your mother's gift—"

"You knew my mother?" Digan croaked.

"In time, you will learn all, my boy," the wizard promised, patting Digan's hand. "For now, let it suffice to know that you will be able to tell your children the story of these adventures with your own words. And to tell this beautiful lady and her esteemed father why you lied to them so shamefully—and what cost you were willing to pay."

Talthos led Allysian forward, and Digan laid the treasured lute aside as she sank down beside him on the soft couch.

The princess threw herself into his arms, and he hugged her to him in wonder. "Oh, Sian," he whispered roughly, "I do love you so!"

Allysian returned his embrace with all her strength. "When I thought I would lose you, I was out of my mind, until the lady Freitanya told me of her plan."

"What plan?" Digan murmured; his throat hurt even more if he tried to speak normally. "Why are you here? Where *is* here?"

"Why, the plan to rescue you, of course! And I am here because I chose to be. I'm afraid *my* wish was a little more selfish than yours."

"But your father—"

"Would gladly have rescinded his order if you offered him the slightest excuse to do so," put in Vasileios from his nearby chair. "The sentence was pronounced in anger, and earnestly repented...but a king cannot countermand his own decrees without due cause, or his word ceases to have any meaning."

"A princess, however, is not quite so rigidly constrained," Allysian added, with a teasing smile for her father before turning back to Digan. "Papa will accept you now, or he will have to find another successor."

"No," said Mordigan, shaking his head firmly.

"W-what do you mean 'no'?" Allysian's lip trembled.

"You will be a great queen," he answered, his voice a mere breath of sound. "I will not stand in the way of that. I have made a mess of my own life, but I will not allow you to jeopardize the future of the entire country for my own pleasure. Don't you see, Sian?" Digan brushed away a tear that was rolling down her cheek. "I have to do *one* thing right in my miserable life."

"Ah, but you didn't let the girl tell you what *she* wished for, young Mordigan," chortled the witch. "She told you it was selfish. Allysian's wish is to have you as her consort before she will agree to accept the throne...and I have vowed to fulfill her wish as I did yours. So, you see, if you do not want her to abdicate her right to rule, you must agree to govern beside her—and if you do not rule beside her, how can I grant *your* wish to take care of her?"

"I—" Mordigan closed his mouth. He could think of nothing to say.

"We will discuss the future later, my boy," Vasileios said, rising to his feet, "but my daughter is unused to being thwarted. I fear you will have no choice in the end. For now, you must rest, and I would like to see more of this glorious city."

"Come away, Princess, and let the boy rest," counseled the witch, taking Allysian's hand. "There will be time enough together later." Freitanya led the girl and her father away.

"I'm glad you are all right, Mordigan Bryre," Gauston murmured shyly, and then followed the others from the room.

Digan lay back on the soft bed, his fingers straying to his throat, which felt like it was bathed in flames.

"I can give you something for the pain," offered Talthos quietly.

Digan shook his head. "It's not—" He started to lie and say "—that bad" ...but if he learned any lesson from this journey, it was the futility of lying. "Necessary," he finished. "Please, sir...you say you knew my mother?" He turned those beautiful emerald eyes on the wizard, and the magic-user nodded.

"She was...my daughter," Talthos murmured.

Digan's eyes widened, and he gulped back his questions, sensing that Talthos needed to continue in his own way, now that he was finally begun.

"I loved her very dearly," the wizard confessed, "as the king treasures Allysian. Her mother died young as well, and Meilora was my entire world. When she was just sixteen, she met a young man—your father—a penniless minstrel with a glib tongue and a ready smile who first came to me seeking a magical lute of his own. They ran away together. It was two years before I could discover where they fled...and two more before I tracked them down. By then it was too late—he lay dead of a fever, and she was dying...

"I was embittered by her desertion, and devastated by her loss. I wanted nothing to do with you—and retreated to my cloud city to brood.

"I almost managed to let myself forget until Freitanya sent you to me. That little minx is sometimes a great deal wiser than she appears."

Digan listened in stunned silence. The wizard's revelations were completely unexpected. *And "little minx" is definitely not the phrase I would use to describe Freitanya...*

Something of his thoughts must have shown on Digan's expressive face, for Talthos laughed. "My little sister amuses herself with her disguises, but she is far less decrepit than she would have the world believe."

"Your sister?"

"Aye, nephew," spoke a rich voice from the doorway, "but believe little else he tells you, for your grandfather is almost as smooth a liar as your father was." Freitanya once more abandoned her haggard aspect, and openly appeared to Digan as herself for the first time. "I have put your beloved and our other guests to bed, Mordigan, and you should sleep as well."

"Please, tell me more about my parents," Digan pleaded eagerly, his voice cracking under the strain.

Freitanya sat down on the edge of the bed beside him. A faraway smile played about her lips. "Ah, I remember well the day your father strolled into the azure citadel like he owned the place—how he found it, no one knew—but Darigan Bryre was afraid of no man and no thing...except, perhaps, your grandfather. From the moment that our Meilora saw him, she gazed upon him with the same love you show for Allysian. But fathers, as you well know, are a stubborn breed."

The witch glanced at her brother, who stood scowling out the window. "Talthos did not take to the notion of your father as a son-in-law any better than Vasileios did to you at first. He forbade them to see each other—which, of course, only strengthened their resolve. When they ran away together, it broke your grandfather's heart. He retreated from the world, and used his spells to search for the lovers.

"Meilora was quite skilled in the Magic herself, and her wards worked for a time...until you were born, and Talthos located them through you. Then his stubborn pride made him delay a confrontation—until his daughter lay dying, with her young husband dead before her, and begged her father to come to her.

"We went—for I was not about to let Talthos go alone and bully her—but we were too late to save Meilora. She asked only that her father care for her son. He replied, and I quote..." Freitanya's voice grew harsh. The look she aimed at her brother's stiff back would have pierced a lesser heart. "'Not until thorns break the clouds and summer rains run uphill. Not—"

"'Until a king's daughter becomes a son and your son a savior,'" continued Talthos in a hollow monotone. "'Not until a liar chooses truth and an honest man lies will I care for your son!'" Talthos turned towards them, his face grave. "I threw every possible obstacle I could in your path, Mordigan, to make sure the conditions would never be met. I gave you the fear of heights; I strengthened your inherited propensity to lie and exaggerate; I made sure you grew up vain and willful, filled with self-importance...but in the end, you bested all the trials placed in your way.

"You proved yourself the better man. If you can ever forgive me for abandoning you then, I would be proud to claim you now as my own."

Digan lay still among the pillows. It was more than he could comprehend at once. "He did love her back, didn't he?" he asked Freitanya softly, his eyes haunted.

Freitanya took his hand. "Oh, aye. Your father loved your mother every bit as much as she loved him—and she gazed at him as you do Allysian.

"You have his looks about you—" she continued, her head tilted to one side like a bird's as she studied his face. "His ebony hair and glittering green eyes—but your soul is hers beneath your bluster. Though Darigan's glib tongue gave Meilora's voice utterance, your mother's heart would not let you truly harm another. You are a good lad, Mordigan Bryre. Are you ready to be a king?"

"I can't," Digan grated out. "I can't be her consort. She needs a royal alliance. The people will accept nothing less. Make her understand—please."

"She will not listen. The child is every bit as stubborn as you are." Freitanya turned to Talthos. "Will you tell him the rest, or shall I?"

Talthos scowled, and folded his arms across his chest. "I was going to tell him," the wizard replied, sounding like a petulant schoolboy.

"When?"

"In good time!"

Mordigan looked from one to the other in bewilderment as they squabbled like children. Freitanya giggled.

"Poor boy," she murmured, "he doesn't know what to make of us, Tal. Don't worry, Digan...our fights are rarely serious. Come along, Talthos—tell the boy the rest. He deserves to know. It is his birthright."

"There's more?" asked Digan weakly.

"When I searched for the runaways," began the wizard, "I found it easier at first to trace Darigan's past wanderings than their present whereabouts. It seems that—although a younger son, and not the heir—he was a prince by birth in his own country. Your heritage is every bit as royal as that of Allysian. This would be easy enough to prove if necessary, but Darigan's brother is king there now, and might not take kindly to a royal nephew appearing to challenge his childless house. What matters is this—if it is merely your lowly birth that stands between you and the girl you love— there is no reason not to accept your place at her side."

Digan felt the room begin to spin. *In less than twenty-four hours I was sentenced to die, struck mute, lost the woman I love, was hung by the neck, found myself rescued by my beloved, regained my tongue, discovered I was kin to the two most powerful magic-users in the kingdom, and now—become a prince by birthright. By Hathor...it is too much.*

Discretion being the better part of valor—Digan promptly fainted.

When he next came to his senses, the room was bathed in the golden light of sunset. Allysian sat beside the window her head bent low over a book. The sun turned her fair hair into a gilt helmet, and limned her features with a nimbus of light. He lay quietly for some time, watching her gasp and sigh over the characters in her book.

At last, as if feeling his eyes upon her, she marked her place in the book and smiled over at him. "Hello, sleepy-head. How do you feel?"

"Better," he croaked, stretching out a hand to her.

Allysian came to sit beside him. "You wouldn't lie to me?" she asked with an anxious frown.

"Never again," he promised.

And Mordigan Bryre kept his word.

ACKNOWLEDGMENTS

THE ORIGINAL EDITION OF this book would not have neem possible without the expert guidance of my *book doctor*, Patricia Gibson, and the finesse of my editor, Ariana Overton. They helped me bring out the best in Digan...or so I thought until Dick Claassen helped me make the book even better.

I would also like to thank Tam for making me visualize Marineaux City...to the point of having created an incredibly detailed town map that had my father the architect shaking his head. Christa, who listened to me read the first draft aloud to her one night and wanted more. Atlanta, who read the next draft on her own one night and *still* wanted more.

Finally, to all those who have helped me shape a phrase here, a scene there.

ABOUT THE AUTHOR

RIE SHERIDAN ROSE MULTITASKS. A lot. Her short stories appear in numerous anthologies, including Nightmare Stalkers and Dream Walkers Vols. 1 and 2, and Killing It Softly Vols. 1 and 2. She has authored nine prior novels, six poetry chapbooks, and lyrics for dozens of songs. These were mostly written in conjunction with Marc Gunn, and can be found on "Don't Go Drinking with Hobbits" and "Pirates vs. Dragons" for the most part—with a few scattered exceptions.

Her most extensive work to date is The Conn-Mann Chronicles Steampunk series with four books released so far: T*he Marvelous Mechanical Man, The Nearly Notorious Nun, The Incredibly Irritating Irishman* and The Fiercely Formidable Fugitive.

Skellyman is her first foray into full-length horror, but she has worked up to it with dozens of horror short stories and flash pieces.

Rie lives in Texas with her wonderful husband and several spoiled cat-children. They keep her busy when she isn't at the computer keys.

Her fan page on Facebook allows fan interaction and offers news and contests:

http://www.facebook.com/pages/Rie-Sheridan-Rose/38814481714
Her newly polished website can be found at:
http://www.riewriter.com
or learn more about the Conn-Mann Chronicles at:
http://theconnmannchronicles.com/
Follow her on twitter at @RieSheridanRose

www.ingramcontent.com/pod-product-compliance
Lightning Source LLC
Chambersburg PA
CBHW022029260626
47156CB00017B/1013